AMERICAN ALICE

Richard Freeborn

Dynasty Press Ltd.
36 Ravensdon Street
London SE11 4AR
www.dynastypress.co.uk

First published in this version by Dynasty Press Ltd.

ISBN: 978-0-956803-82-5

Copyright © Richard Freeborn 2012

Richard Freeborn has asserted his right under the Copyright, Designs and Patents Act 1988 to be identified as the author of this work.

All Rights Reserved. No part of this publication may be reproduced in any form or by any means without the written permission of the publishers.

Cover Artwork and Typeset by Shore Books, Blackborough End, Norfolk.

Printed and bound in the United Kingdom.

American Alice is a work of fiction based on extensive historical research by the distinguished author and academic Richard Freeborn, this is the story of the passionate and unlikely love affair between the American Alice May and a Russian doctor who fall in love amidst the chaos of the bloody Russian defeat by the Japanese in war torn Manchuria.

The war itself clarifies the characters' feelings. It simultaneously increases a reader's involvement in their love, their hopes and their heroism, by demonstrating how military expediency can be overturned in an instant through the heroine's determination to save as many lives as possible.

Alice, suspected of spying even as she nurses the Russian wounded in the American Mission in Mukden, is outraged by the injustice and inhumanity of the Russian commanders and defies all the perils of their defeat to rescue 'her' wounded. Such boldness earns the respect of everyone round her. When the last train from Mukden evacuates the Russian soldiers she is justly acclaimed by everyone as truly an American Alice who has worked wonders to exemplify true heroic endeavour, not grandiose, but essentially life giving.

Richard Freeborn was Chair of Russian literature at the School of Slavonic and East European Studies (SSEES). His published translations include Dostoevsky and the major literary works of Ivan Turgenev. He has written many studies devoted to modern Russian history, the rise of the Russian novel and the Russian revolutionary novel. He oversaw the translation of the screenplay of **Dr Zhivago** for MGM, and **Helen Mirren** and **John Hurt** wrote of their success in his translation of A Month in the Country that it was much 'to do with his wonderful translation' as they had 'lived with his words with such pleasure and fun.'

From this conflict the international prestige of the United States as peacemaker emerged - the Treaty of Portsmouth was signed between the warring parties under President Roosevelt's auspices in September 1905. The dominance of the United States in world affairs can be said to date from that moment.

Written succinctly, clearly, with stylistic care and in a manner designed to emphasize the setting, the perilous circumstances and complexities of the characters' lives, it is their emotional response to the overarching fact of a war not of their making and indifferent to their fates.

Previous novels by Richard Freeborn are *Two Ways of Life* (Hodder, London, 1962), *The Emigration of Sergey Ivano*vich (Hodder, London,1963; Morrow, NY, 1965), *Russian Roulette* (Cassell, London, 1979), and *The Russian Crucifix* (Macmillan, London, 1987; St Martin's, NY, 1987).

For Anne, loving wife, incomparable mother and poet.

In memory of my brother Jack (1930-2011).

1

The train ground to a halt with a scream of brakes. At that very moment a peaked fur hat bobbed up outside like a jack-in-a box, rose to the level of the carriage window and vanished.

Alice saw it, but the central aisle became crammed instantly. Passengers crowded together, officers of all ages, their orderlies, doctors, nurses, the seedier men in fur coats she'd never spoken to, all of them pressing forward with shouts about their luggage into an outside world filled with clouds of steam, blown snow, upturned faces, Chinese porters scurrying along the low platform and cries of greeting as the new arrivals stepped down from the carriage, so that, in wondering what to do next, all she saw were her own dark window-reflected features looming against exterior snowflakes until she snatched her gaze away to confront the peaked fur hat suddenly just beside her in the crowded carriage. Light-blue eyes looked at her out of a square beardless clear-skinned handsome face.

'May I inquire, are you the Reverend Elliott's niece? Forgive me if I... I am the Reverend Gary Edstrom, you see, and I'm mighty glad to welcome you. Are you just arrived from London?'

Alice drew in a breath very sharply. She knew she was unlikely to look like the Reverend Elliott's niece. Intimidated a little by the small silver cross fixed to the fur hat, she did not immediately take the hand held out to her. The young man had drawn off his fur glove. His broad red lips were parted in a genuine American smile of welcome.

'No, I am Alice May. We didn't know who would be meeting us here. The telegram we received didn't say. No, I am escorting them - Miss Elizabeth Wyburn here, who is his niece.' She pointed to a pretty girl seated opposite. 'And his nephew, Oliver, who is...'

She was about to say Oliver was in an adjacent compartment in the carriage divided as it was into separate compartments only by high bench seats but, broad-shouldered though his thick fur coat made him, the young man swung past Alice in over-hasty embarrassment. She sensed the muscular tautness of his body as the coat swung with him. It fitted the slightly forced tone of his deep voice.

'The Reverend Gary Edstrom, ma'am!' The exclamation was challenging. Elizabeth took the newly offered hand and shook it. 'So you are Miss Elizabeth Wyburn just arrived from London?'

'We came via Moscow,' the girl countered, rising to her feet.

'Oh, yes, of course from Moscow! My, what a journey! I sure am delighted to welcome you! God be with you, all of you!'

Elizabeth had taken care to make herself presentable by dabbing on a little powder. It gave her face an attractively porcelain glow, framed as it was in a neat v-shape by the lower rim of the fur hat just above her dark eyebrows and her coat's high, wired collar. She blushed almost despite herself as she withdrew her hand quickly and frowned at her momentary lack of control. Gary Edstrom revealed a head of ruffled blond hair when he removed his hat and repeated his welcome.

'Well, there've been such delays, haven't there. It is my pleasure… Ah!'

A tall fair-haired boy poked his head over the top of the high bench seat separating the compartments.

'Hi, I'm her brother, I'm Oliver!'

'Nice to meet you, Oliver! Welcome to China! I'm afraid I have to welcome you all to a war. But we are not affected. We are neutral.'

Noticing from their faces that he may have misjudged the mood, he checked himself a moment. Instead, half turning, he gestured respectfully to an elderly Chinese man who appeared behind him.

'Here is Mr Wei. Let me introduce him. Our most honoured friend, our benefactor and our aide in all things.'

Mr Wei beamed an elderly creased smile at each of them. He was dressed in a thick quilted jacket and a long garment that looked to Alice very much like a priest's cassock. With slow dignity, his hands in his sleeves, Mr Wei bowed, requested their travel papers, secreted them in his sleeves, bowed again and withdrew.

'Where is your luggage?' Gary Edstrom asked. 'Is it all here?'

Alice said Oliver had been looking after it in the adjacent compartment. The boy echoed this and a glance over the high wooden back of the seat led Gary Edstrom to shout to someone called Vassia out on the platform.

'Is this all of it?'

They agreed it was. It had been piled up in the adjoining compartment throughout the journey from Moscow via Lake Baikal. It required someone as big as the man called Vassia, dressed in thick fur coat and boots, to push his way through the press of alighting passengers and begin offloading all the cases from the train.

'No one mentioned about him.' Elizabeth's excited whisper to Alice was accompanied by her eyes signalling Gary Edstrom.

'Who? You mean…'

'No one said he would be, you know, so…'

'I didn't know who'd meet us.'

'I thought it'd be our old uncle, Uncle Elliott. But he's…'

'What?'

'So good-looking. Isn't he?'

Elizabeth looked away quickly. Gary Edstrom had turned back to them, saying loudly:

'I had no idea! No idea at all you would have had so much luggage! It sure is serious, this!'

Alice could see he was nervy and the reason shortly became clear. He was waiting until the last passengers had left and they had the carriage to themselves. Replacing his hat and pulling on his glove, he looked each of the new arrivals in the eye and ran the tip of a pink tongue round his lips.

'Listen up, please, all of you.' He spoke slowly and softly. 'I know you, Miss Elizabeth, and you, Oliver, won't like to hear this. It's not good news, I'm afraid. Your uncle, the Reverend Elliott Wyburn, would have wished to welcome you here himself, but he is…' another lick of the moist lips '…he is unwell. He asked me to welcome you in his place and I sure am sorry he couldn't…'

'Unwell? What is wrong?'

Alice had no time for the salve of soft words when there was talk of illness. Six months of looking after her sick mother had taught her that. The light-blue eyes of Gary Edstrom surveyed her for an instant. He pressed his lips together tightly and prepared to explain.

'He suffered a heart attack three days ago. It has taken us all by surprise.' He blinked several times and sniffed. 'He was so sure he would take you all to San Francisco. Now, we…' A shrug. 'I am sorry we were not able to contact you. For better or for worse, we thought it best you did not know, because we did not know how severe it was. We still don't know. So you see I can't say how unwell he is.'

'I see.'

Alice realized at once that this news could make the whole journey pointless. She showed her shock by going pale. Elizabeth and Oliver also exchanged puzzled, worried looks with her, but there was no time to say anything because they were being summoned out of the carriage. On the low platform, in a covered area near the station entrance, two Russian officers in long overcoats were scrutinising their papers. Revolvers in shiny leather upholsters fixed to waist belts were obvious signs that the new arrivals had entered a war zone.

A small pony-drawn cart had been brought to the station for their luggage. Gary Edstrom apologised for its inadequacy. Had he known so much luggage was being brought, he would have arranged for another cart to be available as well. As it was, they would have to walk. Unless, of course, he sent Vassia back to the Mission.

'No,' Alice said bluntly, used to speaking for her charges, 'we will walk. Elizabeth dear, Oliver, is that all right? If it's not too far…'

'I am afraid it is a mile at least. I am so sorry. If I'd known… You see, they don't like people loitering round the station.' Gary Edstrom confided in a whisper that the Russians had requisitioned practically all the available carts to move their own supplies. 'It hardly makes them best buddies among the locals, that's for sure. In any case, they think we're all spies.'

'Spies!'

'Ssshh! Try not to behave like one! Just do what they say!'

To have come this far, Alice thought, all the way from London, to be branded as spies! It was quite the silliest thing she had heard. But she obediently waited outside the carriage, as they all waited, stamping their feet to keep warm and hugging their coats close, while their documents were scrutinised, a process that involved Vassia and Gary Edstrom and Mr Wei in what seemed like a prolonged negotiation with the Russian officers, joined by a trio of officials. Their baggage had already been carried out of the train and piled high on the cart, but if 'old Uncle Elliott', as Elizabeth had referred to him, were ill, what was the point in staying here, in this cold, snowy place, when niece and nephew, as Alice well knew, were almost strangers to their old uncle, having seen him only once in their young lives? It was all desperately worrying and puzzling.

Theirs was the only carriage of the long train, the rest being wagons from which troops were alighting and being formed into ranks. Horses were being led down ramps some distance away. It was soon obvious that the presence of civilians was an embarrassment and shortly came smart salutes. One of the Russian officers, with the brightest hazel eyes Alice had ever seen and his fur hat worn at a jaunty angle, introduced himself in oddly accented English:

'Nikki Koz-*lov*, madame! At your serv-*ees*! Wel-*come*!'

She clutched her little handbag to her and tried to smile back, glad they were apparently not spies. A moment later they were herded out of the station under the mistrustful eyes of soldiers with fixed bayonets and watchful local Chinese.

Glad though she was to be liberated from the train, Alice found herself momentarily shoulder to shoulder with Gary Edstrom and could not help herself from mentioning their predicament.

'I am only here because my father begged me by letter and telegraph to escort them here. Their father, you see…'

'Yes, the Reverend Elliott told me,' Gary Edstrom interrupted in a quick whisper. 'You were to bring the children. Your father was Leonard's - that's his brother's – partner, he said.'

'Yes, my father *is* the partner in the insurance business, but he's in New York now. We were all to sail to San Francisco from here and I would then go on to New York. My father was sure the war would be over by Christmas. The Russians would have won by then, he was sure of that. That's just what *their* father thought, too. Before he, you know…'

'Passed on?'

'Yes.'

'Sure, I understand. But things haven't worked out quite the way the Russians wanted, I'm afraid.'

There was no chance of saying more because the moment they were out of the station all thought of future plans were dashed from her mind by the immediate need to hold her scarf tightly over her mouth to fend off the spiky snowflakes that blew like sharp darts against her cheeks. She also found she had to tie her shawl hastily over her head to keep her fur hat in place against the sudden gusts of icy wind. Her handbag clutched in front of her, she resigned herself to keeping her eyes fixed as firmly as possible on the ground.

So they trudged slowly behind the cart along a rutted snow-strewn track lined on either side by small mud-coloured houses. Apart from fences and telegraph poles glimpsed out of the corners of her eyes the only feature Alice noticed especially was a big earth rampart just outside the station. It marked the outer urban limits, so Mr Wei took the opportunity of whispering as he leaned very close in the lee of it. She thanked him, but all further attempts at conversation were thwarted by the wind emerging from the bleak November landscape beyond the houses once the rampart was passed. She had to concentrate on what was underfoot as well as the buffetings from Chinese porters struggling under heavy loads beside her. Ahead of her were Elizabeth and Gary Edstrom and the sight gladdened her. She knew that some kind of spark had been struck at their first meeting.

The continuous wind as well as her stiffness after spending so much time cooped up in the train made it hard to walk fast. Now all she could do was feel grateful that she had bought new boots and had her mother's old fur muff with her. The warmth in her hands seemed to be a token of her mother's enduring love. She could think of her mother again as she had been before her illness, the poised, elegant, socially charming Mrs Helen May who ran the London house so well and had such a fine reputation as a hostess. But that was all in the past, as old as Alice's old overcoat that let the chilly wind in through the seams and reminded her at each step of the increasingly worrying fact that surrounding her, and more chilling than the wind, was a world at war.

They were within sight of the main gate to the old city, so Mr Wei informed her, again whispering but without managing to give it a name she could understand, when war caught up with her. A loud drumming of hooves behind them signalled the approach of a detachment of Russian cavalry. Everyone scattered to the edges of the track as the horses kicked up dust and dry snow and the riders brandished sabres and lances. More horses followed pulling gun carriages, covered wagons, mobile kitchens, creaking closed carriages and carts loaded with stores. The convoy roared past them and disappeared through the gateway beneath an elaborate arch of grimacing dragons.

She was overwhelmed by angry resentment at such an arrogant display of military force. It was a spontaneous reaction to her initial fear. She felt like shouting and shaking her fist, but Mr Wei restrained her by indicating calmly that the universal Chinese reaction was to ignore the whole thing. Instead, to her astonishment, she found as soon as they entered the old city that the Reverend Gary Edstrom and his little party drew solemn and respectful bows from each side of the street. His response was to give little nods and waves of his fur glove. Mr Wei received similar greetings. Alice, as his companion, drew solemn, neutral, blank stares.

Everywhere was noise. The high-pitched clicking talk of shoppers and vendors was as vivacious and incomprehensible to her as the chatter of an aviary. Equally surprising after the bleakness outside the old city walls were the colours and shapes. Banners and pennants, mingled with garments and utensils hung out for display, fluttered greetings of their own in a wind reduced to frolicsome eddies and chill little breezes. Their whirling pirouettes, accompanied by snowflakes fine as rice, matched the ornate decorations on many of the single-storey buildings as well as the flapping awnings of rows of booths. The signs protruding from roof eaves seemed to have the shapes of exotic animals, mainly dragons screaming rigid defiance or frozen into postures of menace. At street level in the market areas the quilted, jostling, talkative crowds went on with their business regardless of the threats posed by the sumptuous red and gold creatures just above their heads.

She pointed appreciatively to these decorations and Mr Wei smiled calmly back at her, gave a little bow, but did not say anything and when she wondered aloud why there seemed to be so few women in the streets he did the same thing. Thinking she might have caused offence, she was relieved when he bowed again and drew her attention to something else.

'*Yamens*!'

This made no sense. In immediate explanation he pointed at some of the buildings. Most looked exactly as she would have expected buildings to look in China and none looked more typical than the majestic orange-roofed imperial palace glimpsed within its own walls at the city's centre.

'Dear lady, permit me. I will explain.' He put his mouth very close to her ear and spoke in slow, impeccable English interrupted by brief pauses as if each group of words deserved formal respect. 'Welcome to...our city... now named Mukden.'

'Thank you,' Alice said equally respectfully.

'Gods,' he whispered, 'only Gods...'

'Pardon?'

'Only Gods dwell... above earth.'

'I see.'

'Men dwell like animals.' A pause. 'Close to earth. So only Gods dwell... in towers. Men, no. Men not dwell in towers.'

'Yes, well...'

She had no idea how to respond to this solemn pronouncement, except she caught the twinkle of amusement in Mr Wei's eye as he turned away from her to admire the ornamented, steeply pitched roofs of so many of the surrounding buildings, quickly turning back to her with an enigmatic expression and surprising her with an equally enigmatic further pronouncement.

'I will explain. We know Gods. Gods are all round us. But we also know... because we are Christian people... about angels. Angels always dwell... above earth. You know angels dwell above earth, yes?'

'Oh, yes.'

'Then angels can dwell... in towers.' With an elegantly polite gesture he pointed out a small church-like building with a tower. 'A small Christian tower, you see, dear lady... for small angels. Excuse me, I am greatly believing... greatly believing in angels. When you will see our Mission, you will see it is suitable dwelling-place... for angels. You will see.'

'Oh, I'm sure. The Reverend Elliott Wyburn... Oh, I'm so sorry he's ill! We've only come here because of him. He's Elizabeth's and Oliver's uncle and their only relative. He was described in my father's letter as being a man of God...'

'Revellend Elliott,' whispered Mr Wei confidentially, 'is angel, real angel. Very, very few people like that, dear lady.'

'Oh, I'm sure.'

'Now we have... very great need, very great need... of angels.'

She could not be sure that he was serious and gave him a slightly puzzled look, only for him to remove his hands suddenly from his sleeves and spread them palm-upwards to the sky.

'Always we need angels, dear lady. Now we need them! Harken!'

The strange Biblical imperative astonished her and once more she was not sure to take it seriously. Then she heard the dull boom. Guns!

'Harken!'

They both paused, as their little procession had paused and everyone else in the street. Borne on the wind was the sound of an unnatural, reverberant thunder. For several moments it sounded quite loud, as if it were only just beyond the city walls, and then it lessened and merged with the flapping sounds of pennants and awnings and the general street noise.

Alice could only be confounded by the contrast between what she had just heard and the busy city enclosed by its walls. Her own successive feelings of discomfort and self-pity and uncertainty and wonder at the strangeness of it all seemed to match the contrast between the decorated buildings and the drab people, between the almost snow-less streets and the outer world of wind-borne snow and gunfire. She had been told there was a war on, but it had always been distant, like practically everything in the newspapers. Though they had seen soldiers and military equipment on their trans-Siberian journey, particularly since crossing Lake Baikal and after leaving Harbin, and she had used such Russian words as she had to strike up modest conversations with a young officer and a nurse in the same carriage, her main concern had been to ensure that she and her charges arrived safely in China, after which Uncle Elliott would take over for the onward journey to Tokyo and San Francisco. Now, though, all that seemed as remote as the moon. Now her only choice was to face what revealed itself to her when she passed through the southeast gate of the old city in the wake of the cart piled high with their luggage.

Set some way down a slope, among a cluster of low-roofed houses, stood the Mission. It was a two-storey structure of pale reddish brick. At first glance the only concession to Chinese tastes was an elaborate covered gateway. The roof of glistening green tiles immediately caught the eye, its colour and design unfairly emphasizing the utilitarian look of the main building with its gleaming rectangular windows and two large white crosses painted on the brickwork as if in demonstration of its clinical efficiency rather than its wartime neutrality.

Below it was a tree-lined avenue leading down to a narrow bridge over the River Hun. As soon as Alice stepped out once again into the cold wind, she saw the convoy and cavalry escort that had raced past them waiting at the bottom of the avenue for a chance to cross the bridge. Groups of Chinese steadily approached up the slope, some humping produce or hauling little trolleys, some evidently families, the swaddled shapes bobbing on women's backs looking so grave-faced and ancient she hardly recognised them as babies. On the other hand, she recognised only too clearly that the congestion down by the bridge was due to a line of vehicles attempting to cross from the other side where, if intermittently, between snow flurries, the distant sky seemed to be smeared with trails of black smoke as if it were so much black ink dissolving in cloudy water.

Momentarily her teeth began chattering. Urged to hurry, she went quickly down to the Mission entrance. Several soldiers in army greatcoats were squatting in the lee of a low parapet wall, all seemed blood-stained, particularly those with bandages visible beneath forage caps. She wondered why Russian soldiers should be there and on an impulse tried asking them, using words she had learned on the train, but the instant she spoke her mouth became filled with freezing cold air.

The men stared at her. One, who may have understood, slowly shook his head. A Chinese girl leaning over a cart glanced up at her. She wore a white uniform and an elaborate nurse's wimple that looked as if it had wings. Alice quickly realized she might be interrupting a medical inspection of some kind and was frankly glad when Mr Wei gently seized her by the arm and drew her away from the soldiers with another of his explanations.

'Our Mission… neutral. Very strict rule.'

She pressed her lips together tightly at his soft-sounding rebuke and nodded.

'Our Mission is open for all, for Russia people, China people, all people. Good medicine is for all people! But…' he raised his eyebrows a little sadly '… Russia people not always pay. And no guns. Very strict rule… no guns. You speak it – Russia language?'

'I have been trying to learn it, yes. I spoke some on the train. Surely, there are Russian hospitals, aren't there?'

Mr Wei conceded there were. But his remark ended enigmatically:

'You see, dear lady, it is not our war.'

'But there must be military hospitals?'

'Oh, near station, yes!' He pointed back to the city wall and the way they had come. 'Here is close.'

She knew at once he meant 'close to the war' and again nodded her understanding. Meanwhile, the already half-open doors to the Mission were opened wide to admit the cart and Gary Edstrom at the head of his little party.

Alice, Elizabeth, Oliver and Mr Wei trooped in to find a small welcoming line of half-a-dozen Chinese nurses dressed in the same winged wimples as the girl outside, who bowed one after another, smiling at each new arrival in turn and then retreating a little to allow two men, one a small, elderly, bespectacled man in a white doctor's coat, and another similarly dressed by much younger, with a head of thick black hair and intense blue eyes, to step forward and shake each new arrival by the hand.

'Greetings and welcome to our dear Reverend Elliott's relatives! I am Dr Francis Rawls,' said the elderly doctor. 'And this is my assistant, Dr Leo Nikitin.'

The latter bowed.

'I am Dr Nikitin. I greet you.'

His Russian accent was quite marked and his bow something of a flourish as he shook hands. It contrasted with the welcome given by a buxom lady dressed in white who seized each of the new arrivals by the shoulders, kissed each solemnly on both cheeks and declared loudly that they were now 'in our American Mission in China and we're mighty glad you've arrived safely! Welcome! We'll do our very best for you!'

Alice suddenly felt so comforted by this greeting she spontaneously yawned. She hid her open mouth with a quick hand movement, but could not deny her relief at feeling that the burden of responsibility for accompanying her charges was now partly shared.

Quite unexpectedly she seemed to have reached a kind of substitute home, for, though war might be somewhere on the horizon, here the internal quadrangle of the Mission building left the rest of the world out of sight and out of mind. It was referred to as a 'yard', an open area about the size of a tennis court dominated by a flagstaff flying the stars and stripes. Although the wind made the flag flap sufficiently to cause a slight echo, it seemed to Alice that the yard's natural condition was an all-engulfing silence. It had, she thought, the tranquillity of a church that should not be wantonly disturbed, rather in the way lines of footprints seemed needlessly to disturb white snow patches among some shrubbery leading towards a small white clapboard chapel with a clock above its arched doorway and a bronze bell hanging from a crosspiece above it.

The presence of this sanctum suddenly made her realize how tired she was, so she did not even notice the time. She merely followed Mr Wei who led Elizabeth, Oliver and herself through a gateway beside the chapel into an open snow-covered space bounded on one side by what looked like a school building and playground and, on the other, by four squat single-storey wooden houses, three of which had their exterior shutters closed. Apart from stables and sheds, the perimeter of the Mission appeared to be an earth rampart similar to the one near the station. Beyond it was the river. The higher ground on which the Mission stood enabled white crosses to be seen beyond the rampart. Vaguely Alice realized that down the slope there must be a cemetery.

'Revellend Elliott's house,' said Mr Wei, pointing. 'You live here now.'

Two young Chinese girls dressed in smart quilted coats beckoned them up steps on to a verandah. Smiling, and with giggles, they bowed, practised one or two words of English, gave little waves to encourage the newcomers through the front door and showed Alice and Elizabeth into a neat bedroom.

'Pliss, pliss.' More giggles. 'We open?'

The girls pointed to wooden external shutters. Darkness in the room made the two beds, wash-stand, table and upright chairs look sinister and hostile. Alice was so overcome by tiredness she saw only the beds and said no, she'd rather sleep. Without even washing, though the girls brought in cans of hot water, she stripped off her top clothes, flopped down on to one of the beds and drew the embroidered cover over her. Nothing mattered to her any longer except the opportunity to sleep and sleep and sleep.

'Mr Edstrom has all sorts of things on his mind' was the last thing she heard Elizabeth say. She could not help thinking it was a mantra repeated over and over in the darkness until the warmth of the bedcover and the room's quietness sent her spinning off into a sleep full of brittle dreams.

Following one after another, breaking off, reforming, remaking themselves and coalescing into so many kaleidoscopic patterns, the dreams left her still in a cramped train with wheels banging in her ears for thousands and thousands of miles. Nothing was any longer regular or familiar or distinct. She heard the banging sounds going on and on through her sleep and what should have been regular, familiar and distinct about them became vague and irregular and rather sharp, reminding her again and again of what she most wanted to forget.

2

The tapping on the door was the night nurse telling her that her mother had died early that morning and she had asked why she hadn't been told at once and the nurse had said she thought it best not to wake her.

Alice was out of bed that instant in a rush to get to her mother's bedroom. The young doctor, Dr Simmons, was just coming out, but inside, kneeling, was the priest in his cassock who rose as she entered. All she wanted to do was scream. But then it wasn't the same tapping. It was all ultra-bright light shining in her eyes accompanied by banging.

There was this woman talking loudly in the bedroom in her ear-splitting voice. Alice sat up, rubbed sleep out of her eyes to see if she were real, and blinking, blinking, thought this loud voice could not be real, but the voice persisted in its insistent American tones, not at all like the voices she was used to in London, until finally she saw her standing there in the open doorway.

'Why, gals, so long as you're here an' bright-eyed and bushy-tailed, you're not goin' anyplace!'

Alice then noticed Elizabeth was sitting upright in the adjacent bed fastening back her hair as, one by one, the window shutters were banged back into place outside by the Chinese girls. It took Alice a moment to realize that Elizabeth had said they were going to San Francisco. The bare whitewashed walls and the few items of furniture shone theatrically bright in sunshine bleached into a pallid white from frost on the windowpanes.

'No, you're not goin' anyplace! Not Stateside, not San Francisco! You're staying right here an' you're helpin' us! You're just who we need!'

The buxom nurse was speaking. She was the one who had greeted them on their arrival in the Mission, dressed as before in a uniform starched firmly over a large bosom. Her strong, matronly features were enshrined in white hair and crowned with a frilly bonnet.

Alice protested. 'Please do not shout! After coming thousands of miles, I do not want to be shouted at! Anyhow, we're here to meet the Reverend Elliott Wyburn…' She was embarrassed at being found in bed almost fully dressed. 'Look, we were very tired yesterday. We had to sleep. And it's very cold.'

Then she paused and added a little defiantly: 'In any case, we're not going to stay here.'

The sharp voice grew quieter. 'Right. So you've come a long way. I understand. No, I won't shout. Gals, my name's Daisy, Daisy Royal. Round here people know me as Nurse Daisy. Since the war…' her hands came together and the fingers knitted into a prayerful clasp '…since the war between the Japs and the Russkies I'm in charge, you see. An' I need all the help I can get!'

She nodded towards Alice. 'What is your name, dear?'

'Alice May.'

'Where are you from?'

'England. But I'm American.'

'Okay, but you got, you know… Pardon me if I cause offence.'

'I'm not offended.'

'So you know… Can I say a dark complexion?'

'A polite way of saying I've got a touch of the tar-brush?'

'Well, no, my dear…'

'Well, I have.'

'Look, dear, you say you're Alice and you're American – American Alice, eh? That's all right by me.'

'If you like.'

'Well, I'll call you that. So what are you, my dear?'

She turned to Elizabeth who replied sharply that she was both English and American.

'Their father was American,' Alice said, 'but they were born in England. And I'm here just as a companion. I have brought Miss Elizabeth Wyburn and her brother Oliver here to be with their uncle, the Reverend Elliott Wyburn. Mr Leonard Wyburn, their father, was ill.'

'Yeah, I heard.'

'My father asked me to help because he was Mr Wyburn's business associate. Then, well… By the way, where is Oliver?'

'He's up in the roof.'

'Up in the roof?'

'Daddy died,' said Elizabeth flatly. 'It was terrible for us. Dear Alice has been so good and helpful. And there is no doubt we'll be going to San Francisco with our uncle.'

She spoke in cut glass English seemingly unaware how haughty and self-confident she sounded, though the tone exactly suited her looks. High cheekbones, wide deep-blue eyes, broad lips and pale complexion set against long brown hair accentuated an exquisite, eighteen-year-old beauty, of which she seemed largely unaware but could use to dazzling effect when she chose.

'Right. Fine'n'dandy. But your uncle, the Reverend Elliott, dear man that he is, I don't reckon he'll be fit, not for a while, not to travel to San Francisco. That's why I thought I'd ask for your help.'

There was several seconds' silence after that. All three of them looked at each other. Elizabeth went on calmly tying back her long hair until it had been formed into an untidy bun at the back of her head.

'Thank you,' Alice said eventually. 'But we need to wash and get smartened up.'

'Right, see you gals later, Miss Elizabeth and you, American Alice! Just remember, you're not goin' anyplace!'

Nurse Daisy Royal swept out of the bedroom and the two Chinese girls entered, bowing. Elizabeth looked across at Alice, smirked and shook her head. They were not used to this, either of them. Alice in particular missed the little comforts of having her own room. Since they would not be staying long, this mattered less than the fact that the Chinese girls unpacked for them, laid out clothes, pressed and laundered where necessary, provided hot water for washing and did all they could to meet every need, provoking Elizabeth into crying: 'Why, it's just like home!' as one of the girls brushed her hair.

But of course there were the unspoken truths between them that Nurse Daisy had exposed in her candid, straightforward query about Alice's roots. She was rarely embarrassed by her darker complexion because few people mentioned it to her face whatever they may have thought in private. Certainly neither Elizabeth nor Oliver had said a word about it, although they knew her great-grandmother had been of Negro stock, as attested by the old faded yellow photograph in the silver frame Alice always kept with her and now placed on the table beside her bed along with a photograph of her parents in a similar style of silver frame. Both photographs proclaimed what she was. She had black roots, the blood of slavery in her veins, but through marriage to white husbands over three generations her family legacy had paled and now her own lightly bronzed complexion and dark-brown eyes were enhancements of open, smooth-complexioned, balanced features in an oval face complemented by twin loops of dark hair either side of it.

The insinuation rankled. She felt aggrieved by it and a little defiant. Most of all, despite her own attempts not to react, she resented what she suspected was a patronising tone that dominated breakfast in the small staff dining room.

It began with Christina Arbuckle being introduced. A spinster in her late fifties, she said she had joined the Reverend Elliott's staff when the Mission was first established and had gradually become responsible for looking after the kitchen and ordering provisions. Because supplies from California had been interrupted by the war, she apologised for not being able to provide a better breakfast.

'Here we have some pineapple pieces. I ordered as many cans of produce as I could when supplies were plentiful.'

'Oh, pineapple! I love pineapple!' Elizabeth was delighted. 'How absolutely scrumptious!'

'Here are some preserves. But I'm afraid we only have millet bread right now. Mind, I do have some coffee. Will you all have coffee? We just aren't used to drinking tea like you folks from England.'

'Why, I just love coffee!'

'And you, Miss May, I imagine you're used to coffee.'

There it was again! The insinuation again, even if unintended. Alice told herself not to be so silly. She joined Elizabeth's appreciative cry in enjoyment of the pineapple, having only tasted it once before, but its very novelty made the breakfast more satisfying than anything they had eaten on their train trip. On the other hand, it brought with it the twofold awkwardness of Christine Arbuckle's announcement that she was leaving for the States the next day and the near certainty that their own onward journeying might have to be postponed indefinitely. This was Gary Edstrom's message. 'Retrenchment', 'fortitude', 'sacrifice' - such words dominated what he had to say, because what had happened at the battle of Sha Ho when the Russians had been defeated and forced to retreat to within only a few miles of the Mission had come as a shock to the American staff. The consul had advised evacuation, so all staff with families had gone, leading to the closure of the school and leaving only Dr Rawls and Nurse Daisy Royal in charge of the hospital wing. The Reverend Elliott's sudden illness had also meant that Gary Edstrom was now alone responsible for the day-to-day running of the Mission, aided where possible by Mr Wei.

Fortitude, on the other hand, had ensured from the outset that the Mission was neutral in the conflict and even-handed in its offer to treat casualties from either side, Russian or Japanese. The ground floor or lower of the two hospital wards (each contained between 15 and 20 beds in normal times) had been set aside for this purpose. In fact, the casualties, naturally enough, were practically all Russian, which was why a Russian surgeon, Dr Leo Nikitin, had been recruited. Whether staff recruited locally were Chinese or Japanese or Russian or any nationality did not matter. They were needed, that was all, because the Mission proclaimed its intention, despite shortage of staff, to remain open and ready to serve all-comers so long as its services were needed.

That was the message signed up boldly at its entrance and one of the principal reasons why it enjoyed such respect among local people and belligerents alike. Practical Christianity had always been the Mission's watchword, although this had not meant that Christian worship was neglected. Indeed, the Mission chapel had been attracting worshippers from among the local Chinese community in increasing numbers since the beginning of the war.

Gary Edstrom addressed most of what he said to a smiling Elizabeth who leaned forward intently to listen to him, her eyes glistening in sympathetic anticipation of every word, and he concluded by referring directly to her situation.

'Well, we know you are here simply en route, as it were, but, well…' a headshake, a sigh '…whether or not you will be able to continue as you intended must depend on your uncle's, the Reverend Elliott's health. He is under the care, er, of Vassia and old Dr Rawls, you see. I can't say when he'll be fully fit. So if you have to stay awhile we'll try and make it as comfortable as possible. There's a problem over fuel supplies, so we can't always guarantee hot water. Small things, perhaps, but bothersome and….'

'I hope, I do hope,' Elizabeth broke in a little pertly, with a slight blush, 'we'll be able to stay a little while.'

'Vassia?' Alice asked. 'Who is he?'

'The Reverend Elliott has had Vassia as his manservant ever since the Russians came here. He is Russian. He speaks a bit of English. Above all, he knows the ropes. He drove the cart yesterday, remember?'

To Alice it was quite plain. They mustn't stay. She had been told in London that the war would be over by Christmas, which was why she had agreed to come to China. Now she found it probably wouldn't. So they needed to book passage from Harbin to Tokyo and San Francisco as soon as possible.

'Oh, yes, oh, yes,' Gary Edstrom agreed on being told this. 'But of course you must see the Reverend Elliott. I mean, isn't he the reason why…'

It was true, of course, that the sole reason for coming to the Mission was to see Uncle Elliott, indeed to rely on him, as had been promised, to pay the costs of their journey to California.

'Of course, yes,' she conceded, 'that's why we're here. But you see we've got to…'

'This morning he was feeling better. A little later, when he's dressed, I know he'll want to see you.'

'Surely we can go if necessary if the lady we've just met, Miss Arbuckle, is going tomorrow? I mean I must go in any case. My father's expecting me in New York.'

'Miss Christine booked her passage months back and her papers are validated, but if you're all travelling on the Reverend Elliott's passport and right of passage, I doubt if it can be arranged all that quickly. And you've got to be *bona fide*.'

'What's that mean?'

'You've got to be confirmed as a member of the Mission staff. The Russians insist on that. Now if the Reverend Elliott's ready, I know he'll want to see you.'

Gary Edstrom did not mention, perhaps wisely as it turned out, how frail the Reverend Elliott Wyburn had become. Maybe it made little difference. The shock came when they saw him. He turned out to be an old man sitting bolt upright in a large leather winged armchair who welcomed his niece and nephew initially with an obvious effort to appear robust but whose voice quavered slightly as he spoke. He tried hard to conceal the weakness by urging Elizabeth and Oliver to tell him about themselves. They knew of course, as Alice knew, that they had only seen each other once, on their uncle's visit to London when Elizabeth was a girl of eight and Oliver barely four.

There he was, though, now, in a large ginger fur coat that enveloped him like an eiderdown, with a red woollen scarf wrapped round his neck and his head covered by what looked like a skullcap with a tassel hanging down the back. White hair stuck out fluffily either side of this headgear and complemented a neatly trimmed white beard and moustache framing a wide mouth with prominent lips. Balanced on his thick nose and a little out of kilter with his curly eyebrows were gold-framed pince-nez. They revealed watery pale-blue eyes caught in little pouches of wrinkles. He looked pale and his cheeks were hollow, yet his expression and the glow in his eyes declared his intention to be as vigorous as possible for the meeting with his young relatives.

They had been directed to sit in upright chairs placed in front of him in a bedroom warmed to hothouse temperatures by a hissing and crackling Chinese stove in one corner. The warmth was welcome after the chill of other parts of the Mission building and the snow outside. The smell, on the other hand, and the stuffiness made Alice reach for a handkerchief. She scarcely wanted to define the component parts of the room's atmosphere, since it was as unfamiliar and indefinable as the many framed photographs hanging on the walls or the shelves lined with books, not to mention a wardrobe and chest of drawers and washstand.

She hid her abhorrence behind her handkerchief and was grateful when the old man broke off suddenly to ask if they would permit him to say a prayer.

'Of course,' she said at once. 'Please say a prayer, sir.'

'I just want to thank the Good Lord for bringing you here,' he explained to Elizabeth and Oliver, 'and to say how mighty, mighty glad I am to have had the opportunity of seeing you and hearing what you've told me. I loved your dear father, my brother Leonard, very much, though, well, we didn't always... So may I say a prayer for us all?'

'Please, sir,' Alice repeated.

His niece and nephew agreed with her. Vassia was standing ready to one side with his hands pressed together and his head lowered. Uncle Elliott at once began.

'Dear Lord, protect us this day and throughout our lives.'

Speaking strongly without any quaver in his voice, as no doubt he had been used to saying prayers in the Mission chapel, he glanced up to see if his visitors had closed their eyes. Niece and nephew took the hint. He continued:

'Protect all who are here with us at this time of strife, protect their loved ones, ensure our safety and show us your inestimable gift of peace. Protect us, dear Lord, from our own fears and pour into our hearts your spirit of forgiveness and love. In this way we may understand better what your purpose is in this life and how best we may serve you in achieving it. Amen.'

'Amen,' said Alice.

'Amen,' Elizabeth and Oliver repeated quietly and uncertainly.

'*Amin!*' came Vassia's deep voice as he crossed himself with a flourish.

'May God be with you,' said the old man. 'Now I must ask our other visitor about herself. Your name...' he reached for a piece of paper and adjusted the pince-nez to read it '...is Miss Alice May, that is right, isn't it? You agreed to accompany my niece and nephew on the journey here and you are, I think, the daughter of my late brother's business associate, yes?'

'Yes, sir, I am.'

'Did you know my brother Leonard?'

'For a very short time. Before he went into hospital. My own mother had recently died...'

'Oh, I'm so sorry to hear that. Please accept my condolences.'

'Thank you. My father had to remain in New York for business reasons. So I agreed to accompany your niece and nephew to the Mission here in China and then travel with you, as I understood it, to San Francisco. Afterwards I would go to New York. I could then say I had gone round the world. Well, almost all round the world.'

Uncle Elliott smiled.

'Sure! Of course you could!' The idea tickled him. 'Almost round the world! That's good.'

The old man took off his pince-nez briefly and then replaced them.

Clearing his throat, he said:

'But now I'm not sure about the rest of your journey – or about going round the world. Because look at me.' He tapped a finger against his chest. 'I am an old man and I'm not well. Of course, your aunt and her children will be mighty glad to welcome you home – in California, I mean. Maybe in a month, God willing, I'll be fit enough…'

It was one of those sentences that had to remain unfinished and his audience tried to avoid looking at him. He, in turn, looked out of the window. Slowly he turned back towards them with his hands open in a kind of supplication.

'But that's not the real problem right now. No, right now the problem is the Russian authorities. They control the railway and issue all the travel documents, you see.'

The statement was so surprising Alice gave a gasp. It was as if a door had been suddenly slammed shut on all her future plans.

'I'm sorry, sir,' she said, 'what does that mean?'

Uncle Elliott again cleared his throat. 'It means, my dear, that only those whom they call the *bona fide* members of the Mission staff can leave Mukden, what the Chinese call Shenyang, in present circumstances. My good friend Vassia tells me this. The Russian authorities were suspicious of you yesterday. Now you must stay here for a little while before they'll give permission for you to travel. Do you understand what I'm saying? It may take a while.'

'Surely they can't!' Alice shot an angry glance at the old man and then apologised. She fought back tears of anger. 'I will have to telegraph my father.'

'They're in charge, you know.' Uncle Elliott placed the palms of his hand together. 'Of course, I know that squeezing might help, but I sure don't want to…'

'Squeezing?'

Oliver had asked the question. His uncle suddenly looked intently at the boy.

'*Squeezing* is bribery, my dear boy. You know you got something of my brother's look. You surely have! You got his fair hair and his jaw.'

Oliver was already taller than his sister and in some respects as handsome as her, with the same dark-blue eyes and well-formed mouth. The only real difference was the barely visible fuzziness on his jaw and a mass of fair hair growing thickly over his ears and the collar of his jacket. It emphasised the extent to which the muscularity of a man's body was beginning to erupt beneath the boyish features and the boyish clothes.

Uncle Elliott suddenly seized hold of his headgear and took it off. 'Have you ever clapped eyes on something like this before?'

'About what you were saying…' Alice tried to say.

'No, sir.'

'Raccoon. See the tail. This is my old raccoon hat. Fits my skull like thick crust pastry on apple pie. You know, boy, you remind me of dear Leonard very, very much.'

'Do you mean,' Alice asked, 'we can't make a booking, can't get tickets?'

'No, my dear, nothing can be booked just right now.'

Uncle Elliott continued speaking to Oliver. 'Why, he was the smartest boy in our neighbourhood. Did he never tell you how he made his first bucks?'

'No.'

Elizabeth echoed her brother's negative. Alice took in a deep breath and sighed. She acknowledged that family history came first.

'When I was already at college I remember him – he was about your age - selling insurance to neighbours of ours in Oakland and making good money out of it. By the time he was twenty he had his own business. Me, I decided I should do something else. I qualified medically and then determined I should treat the spiritual man as well as the physical. So I went back to school. But Leonard – he was all over the world, moving first to Boston, then to London and building up his insurance business. The saddest thing was that, well, Leonard and I weren't exactly true buddies. We were too wilful and, truth to tell, we were kinda restless, going off like we did to different parts of the world. But my dear brother always supported what I was doing here. He helped our funding. And now, what with his passing and this darned war... '

If it weren't for the darned war between the Russians and the Japanese, he explained, springily punching his right fist into his left palm with a small smacking sound, he'd maybe not have been so sick. As it was, he said, again looking out of the window, the choice had been difficult.

'It affected my whole life, everything I am, everything I've ever achieved. You see, my adult life has been devoted to missionary work. I have made it my task to serve God in the only way I know. I became wedded to it, so I have no children save those who have joined me in trying to spread the word of God among my Chinese friends, by ministering to their physical and spiritual needs.'

When he turned away from the window to look at his audience, his features seemed suddenly enlivened by renewed conviction. The smile creasing the edges of his mouth matched the slow, moist recital of his achievement in creating what he called 'the American Mission in Mukden' and left the impression he was running his tongue round some very delicious taste. He accompanied his words with smoothing gestures, as if ironing out invisible creases that occurred in the air just above the level of his fur-covered knees.

'So this is what I made. With God's help and dear Leonard's help and the help of all my friends here in China. It has been slow, sometimes exhausting, maybe on occasion even heart breaking, but I think I've gained the confidence of many Chinese friends here and overcome prejudice, earned respect... I've always aimed to train the local Chinese to do everything for themselves. Then came the war.'

He began wiping the lenses of his pince-nez very slowly with a large white handkerchief. His eyes, as he looked at his audience, appeared to glitter nakedly.

'I am an old man, you see, much senior to my brother Leonard, and my health has been poor recently. Then the ticker...' He paused and swallowed before replacing his pince-nez. 'Anyhow the war has hard lessons for us all. On the advice of the American consul, most of our people decided to go home. Gary, the Reverend Gary Edstrom, a fine young man, for sure, he elected to stay, but he's going to find it mighty difficult running it all by himself. There's only one qualified doctor now – we used to have two, plus an assistant – and one nurse – we used to have four – and just one other, dear Christina, you'll likely have met her. So it looks like it'll be up to my Chinese friends to keep it all going. Until the war's over, of course.'

He raised his chin and smiled. 'You will stay as well, I hope. Then we can join your cousins in California.'

'The Russians'll win,' Oliver assured him.

'Maybe. Maybe not. Maybe the war won't reach as far as Mukden. I don't know what'll happen, my boy.'

The fact of the war naturally dominated their thoughts and their talk. Uncle Elliott could not avoid mentioning Port Arthur and the decision to send the Russian Baltic Fleet halfway round the world.

'See, you cannot go on retreating forever. Eventually even the ordinary Russian soldiers will begin asking why. The greatest secret weapon on the Japanese side, you know, is the Russian desire for freedom, especially as it's the Chinese they're supposed to be fighting for, not themselves.'

Suddenly, in the veering character of his talk, he began speaking about Chinese courtesy:

'I sometimes despair for my fellow Americans, you know. We are children in some ways by comparison with the sophistication of the Chinese. They know what courtesy means. For instance, when you greet someone at your home, you must observe the points of honour. A host must meet a visitor midway between his gate and his door. He must be sure to observe the precedence of north before south and east before west. The host will always keep to the west of the pathway and house door and he must always keep half a step behind his guest, if he can.

'The orderliness of Chinese society and the delicacy of their etiquette are things I have always admired. When you take tea with a Chinese and hold the cup with both hands and bow and place it before him and…' in delicate dumb show, with fluent, controlled movements, he showed what he meant '…and then he rises, lifts the cup, thanks you politely and you both drink simultaneously, taking exactly the same number of sips – why, it's as if you are living a beautiful flower, as if you are creating a lotus! That is civilised living in its purest sense! It doesn't matter that they don't know our Lord's gospel, that they haven't recognised the true path to salvation! No, I never dared teach them the meaning of goodness in that sense. All I have taught is another way to make their lives happier.'

His knack of speaking softly at exactly the right pitch, accompanying what he said with little airy gestures and glancing bright-eyed from one listener to another, made the old man a focus of attention. He encompassed all three of them with a bright ring of words. Alice listened just as intently as Elizabeth and Oliver and was not surprised when his tone became more critical.

'But behind it all, you see,' he said a little later, 'behind the lotus flower, behind their etiquette, are many unpleasant things. *Squeezing*, for instance. We call it bribery, as I told you. *Squeezing* is everywhere in Chinese society. It's endemic, like tuberculosis. Take the average Chinese house, for example, why it defies every known law of sanitation! The floors are earth or brick and the living space is most times filled with smoke from the *kang*, which is where the cooking is done. There is a universal habit of spitting, you know, so the environment is thick with bacilli. Well, maybe I am painting too dark a picture, but good hygiene, good sanitation, good education, good medical care, they're what I believe in as surely as I believe in a Good Lord above, and that is what I've tried, I've striven to offer to our Chinese friends! But, oh dear, how long, how very, very long it takes to get them to see how much better their lives could be!'

'*Sudar'*,' Vassia interrupted, '*dai otdokhnut' khot' nemnozhechko…*'

'Sure, Vassia, my friend, I know! Vassia tells me I need to rest. Oh, yes, I've talked too much. But I've enjoyed myself. God bless you! Stay, please, I beseech you! For a little while! Till, the Good Lord being willing, I can go to California with you.'

It was a plea Alice could not disregard, no more than could Elizabeth and Oliver. Almost as much out of loyalty to her father as to his business associate's memory, not to mention Leonard Wyburn's children, she owed it to stay in the American Mission, at least for maybe a week, at least as a kind of obligation.

Discussing it with Elizabeth, this is what she thought. And if she were to stay, she would have to *do* something, she said.

'We will all have to do something,' Elizabeth agreed. 'I think Mr Edstrom would like it, you know.'

'You're sweet on him, aren't you?'

The girl met the challenge of the question with her head raised in a kind of pre-Raphaelite profile as she directed her gaze out of doors. They had returned to their shared bedroom and Alice had sat down on the bed to compose a message to her father.

'Yes, I like him.'

'Your uncle, what a fine person he is!' exclaimed Alice. 'You must be proud. To have created all this, the Mission, I mean.'

Elizabeth took it seriously. 'Yes, I am proud. I would like to work here.'

Knowing the real attraction was Gary Edstrom, and equally certain that the girl wanted to fall in love, as she had confided more than once, Alice smiled to herself. For her part, she could not deny that the Reverend Elliott Wyburn deserved her respect. She had not been impressed as much by anyone in all her twenty-three years as she had been by him. 'But I must tell my father,' she said.

It was a case of sending a telegram as soon as possible. Once written out in capital letters, she took it to the Mission entrance in the hope of arranging to send it and could find no one to talk to. An elderly Chinese man studied the writing, shook his head and gave no sign of comprehension beyond creasing his yellow features into a smile and shrugging. Noticing this, a Russian officer in a long grey coat whom she remembered vaguely from the previous day approached her and raised his hand to his jauntily worn fur hat with a salute of scissor-like precision and a click of his heels.

'English laid-*ee*, yes?'

'Not really, no. American. I want to send a telegram.'

'Ah, *Amerikanka*! I am Nikki Kozl-*ov*! You are most beauty-*ful* laid-*ee*! Please perm-*eet* me to 'elp!'

The suave, not to say unctuous drawl, and the curious accentuation, held her rigid for a moment, especially as she found herself mesmerised by the brilliance of the young officer's eyes. Before she could explain her real need, she was startled by what she glimpsed behind him. More than a dozen small handcarts were lined up in the entrance, each containing a shape covered in a greatcoat or blanket, some displaying blood stained bandages, others evidently with wounds to their limbs only visible when a white-coated doctor in a hood passed from one to another and leaned over, lifted the coverings, inspected the wounds, asked questions and made notes in each case. The doctor was one of those to whom Alice had been briefly introduced on arrival. Beside him, her frilly bonnet bobbing up and down, was Nurse Daisy, who was herself at the head of a small group of Chinese girls in their curiously winged headdresses and neat starched uniforms.

'Why, American Alice,' Nurse Daisy cried out, 'are you coming to help us?'

Though the entranceway beneath its green tiled roof was wide and could accommodate the line of carts, snow kept on being blown in from outside, alighting on faces and clothes. The officer turned away at that moment and started giving orders to wheel some of the carts into the reception area.

'A telegram to my father,' Alice explained.

'Oh, sure,' said Nurse Daisy, 'Dr Leo here can get that off. Boy, are we busy now!'

Alice looked up to see the doctor's smooth-shaven face below the hood he was wearing, pink lips forming into a tired but polite smile and red-rimmed eyes, bright, greyish, a little worried, studying her a moment before looking at the message she had printed out in large capitals. Then she saw the blood stains on the white coat and the blood-red tinge on the tips of the fingers holding the message.

'You wish to send?'

'I do. Can you?'

He nodded. 'You are... Your name is... May, yes?'

'May, yes. Thank you very much. You will let me know how much it costs.'

'Of course.'

'*Spasibo*,' she said.

At that the smile broadened. The carts were being wheeled along paving stones behind him. He held out his hand.

'Leo Nikitin. I am very glad. *Ochen' priatno.*'

'Alice,' she said. 'Alice May.'

'Alice May.' The repetition brought a smile to his lips.

'May she? Alice may, may she?' It was an old joke, but she did not resent it when he took her hand and shook her cold fingers so firmly they suddenly grew blazing hot. She could not help it. She felt herself crimson, even though her complexion did not show it at once, and glanced away, his fingers still holding hers. There was something in his face she could not exactly define. It excited and amazed – a statuesque handsomeness, an immobility of expression, as if the contours were cut neatly from some greater whole and shaped to represent manliness. Then the symmetry dissolved into creases of pleasure round the glow of the eyes.

'You're coming to help us!' Nurse Daisy cried. 'I can see that!'

3

Dr Leo Nikitin swilled his hands in the icy basin water after using the carbolic soap and shook free as many drops as possible. He accepted the towel held out for him.

'Time to go, eh?'

He glanced sideways at the small man beside him who was dressed similarly in white medical garments, a facemask and round spectacles, with little to be seen of his sallow features save two equally round, very dark eyes. The small man nodded.

'Suppose. Yes.'

'So we must do what we must do. *Poshlee, poshlee!*'

Leo Nikitin knew as he spoke that he did not mean exactly what he said and the small man knew equally well that the formal exchange was a sort of code to which only he had access. They entered the operating theatre side by side. It was the pride of the Mission, only recently installed. The operating table was adjustable, with specially designed reflecting oil lamps above it that hissed softly while spreading a diffused bright light. Shiny instruments laid out in a neat row on a wheeled table gleamed alongside the controls of gas cylinders.

The patient was wheeled in and two Chinese orderlies laid him carefully on the operating table. He was naked except for a sheet spread across his lower abdomen and loins. Injuries to his right leg had left burned flesh, shattered bone, lurid scorch marks and hideous lacerations to his forearm and elbow that caused the skin to hang in threads. One of the nurses fainted at the sight.

'Glory to God! Takeo-san, we must work hard.'

Dr Nikitin had spoken. He broke into Russian as a nurse began swabbing iodine over the shoulders and neck of the burly, bearded patient who emitted deep-throated whimpers through teeth gritting a short length of rubber tube. As he heard the doctor's Russian words he stopped rolling his eyes wildly from side to side.

Meanwhile, straps were placed across his chest and his left leg was held down firmly by the two orderlies. The small man wearing spectacles immediately began inserting thin steel pins into the iodine-coated shoulders and neck before quickly and deftly setting to work on the man's injured elbow and forearm. The whimpering grew louder for a moment and then gradually calmed as Takeo-san worked. He was so brisk it was like watching the fingers of a concert pianist flying over the tortured limb. The pain seemed to lessen with each flickering touch.

Simultaneously Dr Nikitin inspected the wounds to the leg and knew he had to perform an amputation. They were all too common now, these traumatic injuries from Japanese artillery, so the procedures for amputation were all too dreadfully familiar. A tourniquet, naturally; the administering of a chloroform drip or ether or gas, surgical spirit on his hands. The doctor worked quickly to flense and retract. A neat severance of the lower thighbone was accompanied by as little loss of blood as possible. Dr Nikitin staggered away from the operating table and Takeo began the delicate task of sewing up the wound.

What Leo Nikitin hated most of all was the feel of warm blood on his fingers, the blood of his own people. He felt it often enough these days but could never get used to it. As he turned once more to the basin and swilled his hands for the umpteenth time that day, he found himself clapped on the shoulder. Looking round, he faced the elderly, smiling eyes of Dr Francis Rawls.

'Have a rest! You've done enough, my dear Leo! We're going to turn away the rest out there. After all, we're here to look after the local people and we can't... we can't divert too much of our energies to your wounded. There's got to be a balanced approach.'

What exactly 'a balanced approach' meant, Leo Nikitin could not be sure. He had been attached to the Mission hospital precisely because so many Russian wounded had been admitted and it was his job to do his best for them, warm blood or no warm blood. The situation was getting worse; and he was tired, dog-tired. He looked out of the window. Snow whirled about between the Mission and the houses and made him feel slightly sick. He lowered his facemask.

'Sure.'

Inside the Mission he could at least feel relatively secure. Out there was nothing but a maelstrom of snow and war. For the moment, to be an equal, to be American and talk English however poorly glued together by the thick-packed consonants of his Russian birth and all the inhibition of being foreign, was, dammit, better than being out there. He would stay with it if he could.

The patient was being bandaged. He had stopped his whimpering. God knows if he would recover. Maybe the shock would be too great. Leo Nikitin tore the white medical hood from his forehead, freed his thick black hair, splashed freezing water over his face and gasped in as much of the carbolic-smelling air as he could before saying thank you to the theatre staff and retiring to his small room on the floor above. There he uncorked a vodka bottle and gave himself a stiff drink. Takeo-san came in behind him shortly afterwards but would not share the drink.

'You win,' Leo Nikitin said.

'Nobody win.' The small man sat down in the only other wicker chair and clasped his hands together in front of him. 'I not wish win.'

'Sure, well... You know what,' said Leo Nikitin. 'I want to go to America. You win, I go to America.'

Takeo nodded and permitted himself a smile. 'I win, *we* go.'

So maybe it was settled by that. Perhaps, years later, looking back on it, they decided that was the first and only moment they spoke of it directly.

'So you win and we go. But Reverend Elliott, will he go?'

'Suppose. No.'

'Takeo, my friend, you are right. But his relatives...' Leo took a swig of the vodka '...girls who came yesterday, they must go. Who wants to stay here when there is possibility to go to America?' Takeo-san nodded so vigorously the straight fringe of black hair on his forehead lifted and fell like a lid. 'It is stupid, young persons like that here! Stupid!'

Again Takeo-san nodded. Leo Nikitin clicked his tongue. He had to ask himself exactly why he was here. Reverie consumed him for several moments. He had nothing to keep him in Mukden except the orders of the imperial medical corps and the sense that he had to help the victims of war as much as possible. His father was dead; his mother an invalid being looked after by two younger sisters and a younger brother (though the boy was only seventeen). He had not seen them for five months. He was no combatant in any sense. As for his ambition, future hopes, even wishes, he had become certain that all his training and the sacrifices made for it, not to speak of his recent experience at the Mission in Mukden, pointed to the need for one fundamental, irrefutable thing: change, political change, fundamental change.

'What is it, Takeo, my friend? War, what is it? Two emperors, two empires, eh? We fight because of two emperors and two empires. Soldiers die, lose arms, lose legs... Why? Do they vote to die? Do they vote to lose arms and legs? Can they vote? You know what it is – *vote*?'

'Oh, yes. In Amellica they vote.'

'In America they vote. You are right. If we vote, well...'

Then he stopped. He knew he was talking to himself. Who were *we*, after all? Was it just he and the small man still in his medical whites sitting opposite him who smiled back so placidly? He always looked as if he were smiling. Was he really smiling? He had never known Takeo-san look as if he wasn't smiling. Ever since their first meeting here in the Mission two months ago, when he had first arrived as an assistant surgeon, he and Takeo-san had somehow been drawn together in a strange friendship of opposites, of Russian and Japanese, of enemies, of secrets and confidences, because he, Leo, had guessed that this neat, efficient, small man who always passed so easily as Chinese and was so expert at acupuncture was not what he seemed and could never be. Treachery of sorts, even consorting with the enemy, had perhaps cemented their closeness, but more assuredly it was mutual respect, a bond forged in working together and based on the shaky but pliant foundation of the readiness to talk to each other in a language neither of them knew too well. So they had always communicated in English. In an American Mission what else could they do?

Leo contemplated the spines of several books on a shelf fixed to the wall. Medical texts rubbed shoulders with Pushkin's poems, Dostoevsky's novels and Tolstoy's *War and Peace*. The gold lettering on the spines of the last two volumes now caught the afternoon light and reminded him in an odd way of candlelight shining in his sisters' eyes. Nostalgia sent a momentary chill to the nape of his neck.

'You said *Poshlee*, yes?'

Leo blinked and nodded, a little surprised at the question.

'It means we go, yes?'

'We go,' Leo agreed.

Takeo-san heaved a very deep sigh and raised his eyes to the ceiling. 'I know. I must go. One week. Two week. From now…some…days.'

A smile perched itself on Leo's lips with the uncertainty of a bird alighting on a telegraph wire. 'Yes, I must also. My emperor has said I must, your emperor has said you must. Things to be done, things to be done! Miss Maddocks, my English teacher, always said: Things to be done! So we have things to be done.'

He knew what he was saying right enough, just as he knew what his friend meant when he said he must go. They would be doing their different things for their country, as patriots, it would be supposed, and preserving their souls as best they could. If they ever met again afterwards, they would very likely have assuaged their consciences to some degree. Leo said:

'You will go back to Tokyo?'

It was strange and unexpected that he should have asked this question. Takeo-san looked down at his hands, still clasped in his lap.

'Suppose. But not know. Maybe it will be…' Each word received its own space as he enunciated very slowly:

'…Maybe…it…will…be…like…you.   Like…I …said.   Maybe Amellica.'

Leo smiled to himself and shook his head.

'Copycat.'

The quietly spoken word puzzled the Japanese.

'What is it?'

'Good,' said Leo. 'So we will meet there, eh?'

Takeo-san understood and beamed a smile. 'Yes, we meet… in Amellica. But now…I say Good Day, Dr Leo.'

Leo waved his hand as the other rose and bowed. Their encounters had always been short.

As the door closed on the Japanese, it occurred to Leo that he had never discovered so much as his friend's real name. They had simply become friends out of sheer propinquity and necessity and the less they knew about each other's motives or past the better. The names he had to know were those of the wounded whom he treated each day. He studied the list a moment, wondering if his friend did the same.

Having removed his medical coat, still flecked with fresh blood as it was, he washed, put on a clean shirt, necktie and waistcoat, pulled on his formal jacket and finally dressed himself in the thick fur coat and hat that had served him so well during the start of the Manchurian winter. It was time for him to make his daily trip to the middle of town. The routine was as much a military duty as a means of temporary escape from his medical responsibilities at the Mission, although he combined several activities, both covert and outwardly respectable, in these little trips of his.

Down the stairs he went, past the clinic entrance now full of local Chinese, past the bay set aside for wounded and the gatekeeper's office and through the single doorway in the main gate into late afternoon dusk and very light stinging snow blown wildly about in a northerly wind and houses crouched low as if hiding from it. Local people were about but scattered, shapes passing him or ahead of him, presences.

Reaching the city gate, he was in two minds about the Russian sentries stationed there who recognised him and saluted, but he was glad of the chance to walk almost unhindered along paved streets protected from the harsher wind by the city walls and less crowded now at the approach of evening due to the curfew imposed at nightfall. Here, in the shadows of the buildings and down alleyways that he knew well enough, he felt himself inconspicuous despite the way the thick fur of his coat and hat enlarged him and made him so obviously bigger than the majority of locals. There were certain people he wanted to see before going to the Dragon Throne hotel.

He tugged at the bell-pull. Maybe somewhere inside the unlit building the sound resonated though he had never heard it in all his visits. It took at least a minute for his summons to be answered. He stood where he knew his face could be seen, illuminated for an instant by a jet of light shone through a spy-hole in the solid wood door. Then it opened. He entered quickly, passing into near darkness before a farther doorway composed of thick slats of wood suspended from a low beam offered access to a dim corridor down which he found himself following a black-haired young man carrying a lantern whose ankle-length coat was composed of leather and creaked almost as loudly as his wooden footwear clattered along the tiled floor. Next was another door, this time unlocked from inside by some signal from the young man. Suddenly they were both in a relatively well-lit workroom with glass-fronted vestibules or offices along one side and in the centre several hand-cranked printing machines busily in motion at that moment. Paper sheets delivered from them were being deftly clipped on to what looked like clotheslines running on pulleys round the ceiling.

The noise, the ink-impregnated air, the dust and cramped conditions, made breathing hard. Leo was glad to be directed as usual into one of the vestibules that was curtained off and lit by an oil lamp perched on a table. Two men rose from behind it as he entered. They clasped him successively in warm embraces, planting kisses on both of his freezing cheeks before a word was spoken. He responded by slowly pulling off a fur glove and extracting from an inside pocket a safe conduct document contained within the small window section of a leather wallet. From behind this document he carefully drew out another sheet of very closely written paper barely larger than the size of his palm.

This he handed across. One of the men instantly sat down as close as possible to the oil lamp and perused it through a magnifying glass. No one spoke. The noise of the printing presses came in clattering waves from the other side of the curtained glass. Then the perusal was over and the magnifying glass placed on the table.

'*Otlichno, Lev Nikolaevich! Otlichno! Nuzhna, v kontse kontsov, kakaia-to... nu, podpis'. Znaete?*'

Probably, Leo thought. A name, a signature, would have to be appended, otherwise it would be thought to be just another scrap of paper issued in the name of the High Command or some other official organisation that no one would read before using it to wipe a nose or a bottom. He carefully replaced the safe conduct document in the wallet.

'Let's see first...' he spoke in Russian '...let's see what effect it has. The distribution, how will that be? Through your network?'

'Oh, yes, oh, yes,' said the man who had perused the sheet. 'It will be distributed. What about that American Mission, can you distribute through that?'

'Very unwise,' Leo said. 'I mean...'

'Yes, yes, I understand. No, no, that mustn't be touched, I appreciate.'

'But if nothing comes from there and from everywhere else,' said the other man, 'won't that seem suspicious?'

Leo was thoughtful. It was easy enough to draft the appeals to a largely peasant army, based as they were on so many little details of military stupidity and injustice gleaned from wounded in the Mission hospital wing, but the need to wrap the manifest truth in conspiratorial secrecy seemed unnecessary, if not irrelevant, at such a time. He knew he should fear for his own future if the true authorship of these leaflets became known, but there was always the strangely comforting axiom, often told him in boyhood, that Russians were a *riskovii narod*, Russians liked taking risks. Maybe the twentieth century would see the whole Russian nation risking itself for the sake of some political ideal. All he said was:

'Maybe. Right. From the Mission as well, if you like.'

Then the first man rose from the table, smiling. He had a little pointed beard that lifted slightly as his lips parted. He looked up into Leo's face.

'The *zemstvo* leaders have demanded a legislative assembly. Did you know?' he whispered. 'It will be revolution otherwise. Things are beginning to change. They will change very, very soon.'

It had all been said before and Leo had heard it before.

'Do your best,' he said. 'I must...'

'You are going where, Lev Nikolaevich?'

'You know I must report to the High Command. I have performed God knows how man surgical operations today. I must be trusted by the High Command, you know, so I must report the names and details of each one... as best I can.'

The two pairs of eyes studying him, shaded momentarily by the backlight effect of the oil lamp, seemed mistrustful. Then the man with the pointed beard clapped him on both shoulders.

'Good. You do well. A good comrade. Give us ammunition. We will fire the guns.'

'My bullets will not kill,' Leo said.

'They will kill the generals, they will kill the Tsar. That's all we need.'

It was enough, he supposed, though Leo took no pride in thinking of his clandestine work as ammunition of any kind. Change was certainly essential and he contented himself with thinking he contributed to such change by drafting these little bulletins that he had learned to compose in the tiniest of handwriting. With a shrug of the shoulders he acknowledged the proffered compliment.

'Very well,' the pointed beard continued, 'till next week, Lev Nikolaevich. Till next week.'

So the routine procedure was followed. It meant that Leo Nikitin was directed out of the building by a different way, through the drying room and the little bindery, past a dozen or more Chinese engaged in preparing newsprint for delivery once the curfew was lifted the next morning, and then into small ill-lit courtyard filled with tarpaulin-covered heaps now glistening white in parts where the snow had eddied. This was a preliminary to entering a crowded and smelly restaurant through which he had to pass before re-entering the street, by which time he had ceased to be clandestine and had become just another Russian civilian occupier of Mukden for whom the curfew did not count.

A foot patrol came down the street. He expected to have his papers scrutinised, but he was not stopped. The fumes of cooking in the restaurant had made him hungry. He looked forward to eating once he had reached the Dragon Throne hotel, even before handing in his report as he knew he should, until suddenly, as if his heart had stopped, he felt overwhelmed by tiredness amounting to exhaustion. He even thought he might fall. For a moment or so the side of a shut market stall offered him support and a chance to rest. Scurrying under his feet told him there were rats. Though he hated the creatures, he felt too tired to be bothered by them.

It came as a shock to realize that he had overworked himself and needed to take greater care if he were to do all the things that had to be done, as Miss Maddocks had always taught him. Of all the women in his life, including his mother and his sisters, it was that tall, thin Englishwoman with the warm smile and the soft voice whom he had probably loved more than any.

The hotel's reception hall was filled with officers, their mistresses, camp followers of various kinds as well as the usual clutch of well-dressed foreigners engaged in 'business' or 'diplomacy' or 'reporting' and mostly now ready to forget there was a front line scarcely more than a dozen miles away. A small balalaika band strummed away vigorously on a miniature stage at the far end of the reception hall and waiters rushed from table to table with shoulder high trays, depositing bottles here, glasses there and *zakuski* wherever needed. A couple of unduly large and somewhat incongruous candelabra hanging from specially installed metal joists in the ceiling provided the lighting as well as some of the heat, but the real source of heating were Chinese stoves placed at intervals round the hall. It was stifling as a result. The steamy, complex miasma had a feel, both familiar and subtly hostile, that Leo automatically associated with his compatriots. It did not surprise him at all to find many of the women had slipped clothing from bare shoulders and men had divested themselves of their tunics. Two young officers, both red-cheeked and streaming with sweat, were busily dancing a Russian dance immediately in front of the balalaika band, egged on by onlookers who clapped and shouted in rhythmical accompaniment.

His fur hat and coat were taken from him as he entered. He was known, though he could not tell who recognised him; perhaps it was one of the bowing waiters who greeted him with a '*Bonsoir, monsieur*' and explained he *did* have a spare seat '*Mais je ne sais pas si vous...*'

Hesitantly, still bowing, hips swaying, he conducted Leo to an empty chair and a space at a round table already occupied by a party of young officers and a dark-haired girl with a pretty, rouged face and scarlet lips who broke into loud laughter at some remark by a companion the moment Leo was seated. Somehow this laughter and all the forced, artificial, drunken gaiety round him seemed oppressively trivial. He stared down at the patch of white tablecloth in front of him and felt tears pricking his eyes. He knew his hands still smelled of the carbolic and surgical spirit, that he was out of place in such surroundings, even alien to the whole atmosphere of the place and its enjoyments, yet this was where he had to come if he were to be classed as 'loyal' and acceptable to the High Command.

A fragrance much pleasanter than the ubiquitous harsh odour of Russian tobacco unexpectedly filled his nostrils. He looked round to see the man beside him straighten his back after stooping to pick up a fallen napkin. He took a lighted pipe out of his mouth.

'You are from the American Mission, I think?'

Middle-aged, lightly bearded, in a tweed jacket, the pink, creased, amiable face of an Englishman whom he had met two, maybe three weeks earlier in this very place leaned towards him.

'Tired?' Leo acknowledged as much. 'You look it. I imagine you have been seeing the worst part of it.'

There was no need to be too explicit. They both knew what was meant.

'No one' - the other stuffed a notepad quickly into an inside pocket ' – no one expected it would be as bad as this. No one.'

Leo recognised him now for what he was, a correspondent of the London *Times*. He agreed with him. A waiter sidled up and requested an order at the very moment that a large bowl of steaming soup, a Mukden version of Russian *borshch*, was set down in front of his neighbour. It was the *plat du jour*, he was informed, ladled instantly from a large tureen. A carafe of vodka accompanied it. Both started eating.

'You have the responsibility, eh?' His neighbour was speaking after several mouthfuls. He had a clipped English accent. Leo looked at him. '…of picking up the pieces, don't you? And the pieces must be pretty grisly.'

Between mouthfuls Leo tried to work out what the word 'grisly' meant. In any case, with all the noise from the other side of the table, he wondered if he had misheard. All he heard next was the statement:

'…the reason, I suppose, why we find ourselves in the presence of such Bacchic revels. Making hay, as we English say, while the sun shines. Do you not agree?'

Leo smiled sourly. The sun had not shone warmly since he came to Manchuria, but echoes of Miss Maddocks's sentiments filled his mind and pierced the readiness of his Russian soul to dwell on death and grief as normal accompaniments of life. He swallowed more of the soup, offered a toast with the vodka and bit into a slice of millet bread.

'No, no, thank you.' The other nodded a polite refusal.

'So,' said Leo, raising his glass to his mouth and tossing back a tot of vodka, feeling there was no need for social reserve, 'you understand *us*, yes? You understand us Russians?'

'Understand?'

'You understand us - Russians?'

'No.' An amused shake of the head. 'No, I admit it – candidly – no, I don't. Enlighten me. Please enlighten me.'

How characteristic, Leo thought with a spurt of annoyance, that this Englishman should be so presumptuous.

'We take risks. Russians take risks.'

'You speak very good English, you know. Where did you learn it?'

'I learned it from Miss Maddocks.'

'Who was she?'

'She taught English. My father wished to read English books. She taught us English. You notice my English is correct, yes? Taught, not teached. Not regular verb.'

'Irregular. Quite right. I imagine you - how can I put it? – you have a foot in two camps, as it were, being Russian, speaking English, working in the American Mission… Do I make sense?'

Leo confronted the somewhat lustreless, intelligent, amused eyes of his neighbour for a moment before returning to his *borshch*.

'Yes,' he said between mouthfuls, 'you make sense.'

'Then let me get something off my chest. No one seems ready to acknowledge that you, the Russians, are engaged in something that will never be to your credit. True?'

Leo nodded.

'So?'

The Englishman gave a faint chuckle.

'I have visited a lot of places on this planet but I have never known deeper sedimentary layers of futility than there are in Russia.'

The laughter from the other side of the table almost drowned out what he was saying and Leo leaned closer to him.

'Do you know what I mean - futility?'

Leo nodded again.

'I don't want to pass judgement on one belligerent as against another, but if… if, on the one hand, you have a predominantly peasant nation and, on the other, a well-trained, militant and highly disciplined Far Eastern nation like the Japanese – well, the answer is not hard to predict. First, the Russian fleet in Port Arthur is disabled. Then you find yourselves outmanoeuvred and defeated again and again on land. Then there is the battle of Sha Ho and you retreat.'

'So?'

'You have only one hope now of remaining in Manchuria and keeping a Far Eastern empire - to construct a defensive line south of Mukden and try to withstand all the Japanese attacks until the Baltic fleet is able to sail round the world, relieve Port Arthur and reinforce what remains of your Far East fleet in Vladivostok. It's a curious strategy but it's the only one left. Am I wrong?'

'Probably not.'

'I just wonder, you see, what drives thousands of Russians over thousands of miles to expend thousands of tons of high explosive fired through hundreds of guns to defend a part of China that is not theirs against an enemy they do not really know.'

He tamped down the tobacco lightly in the bowl of his pipe and relit it with a match that left a small smudge of blue smoke behind it.

'I'll suggest to you what the real reason is, eh?'

'What?'

'The railway south from Harbin is the sole tangible reason for this war. Whoever controls the railway controls Manchuria.' He spoke through a little cloud of fresh tobacco smoke. The smile forming on his creased, amiable face was savage, knowing and hard-bitten. 'That is what makes this war so futile and so cruel.'

'So,' said Leo, 'we make – what is it you say? – *hay*?'

He found his gaze caught at that instant in the shining eyes of the girl opposite as if in a spotlight and for several moments, despite the drunkenly earnest way a young officer whispered in her ear, she fixed her eyes on Leo and began to smile, more at what she saw, it seemed, than what she heard, and he acknowledged her smile by smiling back. It was, he knew, the kind of communion of eyes, of fondness, even of mutual passion that he had sensed for the first time in months when he had looked into Alice May's eyes that morning at the Mission. Shame as well as sexual electricity shot through him at that instant. The girl tossed back her hair and immediately got up, followed by her escorting party. Watching her disappear, he felt at once in his jacket pocket for the message he had promised to send.

'Help me, please,' he begged his companion. 'I forgot something. Please can you send this message?'

The blood-stained note amused the Englishman.

'New York. Of course. So the lady is staying, is she?'

'Yes.'

'Right, I'll send it out tonight.'

There was scarcely time to express thanks before a more familiar, less welcome face peered down at him.

'Ah, Lev Nikolaevich! My dear friend, Lev Nikolaevich!'

With an elaborate flick of the wrist an officer waved a long-stemmed cigarette holder in the air, creating an arc of grey-blue tobacco smoke. He bowed to Leo and his neighbour, each time clicking his heels and giving a salute with fingers curved to the side of straight temples below stiffly pomaded fair hair.

'So I see you are with our enem-*ee!*'

'Yes, Kozlov,' Leo admitted, 'English. Correspondent of English *Times*.'

'Yes, we *know!*'

Among Captain Nikki Kozlov's idiosyncrasies was a tendency to stress the final syllable of each word whenever he spoke English. The affectation matched the pretentiousness of waxed moustaches and cigarette holder that endeavoured to lend maturity and an air of sophistication to a face otherwise dominated by still boyish fresh pink cheeks and bright red lips. His eyes, of purest light ochre, were so glistening and innocent they imparted an attractively candid self-confidence. To Leo he looked exactly as a young aide-de-camp of the Russian High Command should look. The effect was not really militaristic so much as youthfully debonair until one noticed the immaculate uniform jacket nipped in by a shiny belt and revolver holster.

'Per-*meet* me.'

He took the vacated seat opposite them, crossed his legs and stubbed out his cigarette with a small sizzling sound in the remains of some soup.

''Ees imperi*all* Madjest-*ee,*' he began.

'Who?' asked the Englishman.

'Ver*ree* secr*et.*' he confided.

He ran the tips of his fingers with an elegant movement along the curve of his moustaches and admitted he had been on a mission to London only a month previously.

'Ab-*out* our enem*ee* Yell-*ow* Per-*eel.*' He shook his head sadly over the plight of England. 'Great pitt*ee* about Ingl*and*! Ingl*and* supp-*orts* Djap-*an*. When we win war, Ingl*and* will lose face! Yes?'

The Englishman gave a loud sniff.

'You must send des-*patch* back to Lond-*on*, sir. You must say: We will win! Yes?'

'I try to report the truth as I see it. If you win, I will report it.'

'But Americ-*ans*, what do Americ-*ans* think?' he asked Leo.

Leo leaned back and placed a hand in the same pocket from which he had just taken Alice's message.

'They see we have many Russian wounded…so what do you think they think? Here! I have this for you!'

He waved a sheet of paper loosely in front of Nikki Kozlov, who smiled coldly.

'Djap-*an* arm-*ies* much more wound-*ed*! Much more!'

'It is futile, this sort of talk,' said the Englishman.

Nikki Kozlov screwed a monocle under his right eyebrow. He smoothed out the sheet of paper and looked carefully at the list of wounded who had been treated that day in the American Mission.

'*Da, da. Poniatno.*' He refolded the sheet and pocketed it. 'I am grate-*ful*, Lev Nikolaevich. Very grate-*ful*. Tomorr-*ow* I will vis-*it* again.'

Unscrewing the monocle, he then surprised them both by pouring vodka into a glass and holding it up for a toast.

'Two young laid-*ies* arrive yesterday, yes? Very prett-*ee* young laid-*ies*, yes? I propose we drink to laid-*ies*, yes?'

4

'Then my mother died.'

She forgot Elizabeth was there in the bedroom with her and had fallen into a daydream about the time she had spent nursing her mother and waiting for the young doctor's visits. Once he had kissed her. She had sensed all the time the neat fit of his waistcoat and the way his trousers stretched so tightly over muscular thighs as he sat next to her.

'What?'

'I'm sorry, I shouldn't have... It was...' Alice waved her fingers in the air as if she were clearing away cobwebs.

'Your mother died. Yes, Alice dear, you said. I suppose...'

The bedroom was, as usual, cold and they were both dressed for their work, Alice looking down at the photographs of her great-grandmother and her parents in their silver frames and Elizabeth looking at herself in the mirror on the wall by her bed.

'Otherwise you wouldn't have been able to come here with us, that's what I mean. And if Daddy hadn't...' The remark was hurriedly spoken and Alice glanced round.

'I was just, you know...'

Alice tried to remember exactly why she had remembered the young Dr Simmons, why, indeed, she was here in this cold bedroom, until it dawned on her she was stuck here, sharing the bedroom with Elizabeth.

They had just finished lunch. It had stopped snowing but the sky was overcast. Vaguely, distantly, like a voice heard through mist, the clock on the Mission chapel chimed the half-hour.

'You know, I think I'm in love with him,' Elizabeth said after a pause.

'Should I be?'

As if anyone could really answer such a question. She was still studying herself in the mirror. It was characteristic of her to be so self-regarding.

'Of course, you should be! Why on earth not? He's very good-looking, sensible, conscientious...' Alice racked her brains in praise of Gary Edstrom '...very much respected, a good manager, so everyone says, and he's made you his assistant. He's obviously fond of you! I'm sure he'll be kind. Kindness is the main thing. He's a very nice, kind man.'

'What about...'

'What about what?'

'You know - passion? Do you think he has passion?'

Oh, dear, such questions! Alice was emphatic.

'Yes.'

'I'm not sure,' Elizabeth murmured. 'You smell, you know, dear. It's that uniform.'

'I know. I'm sorry. I've got to wear it. Surgical spirit and carbolic and stuff. Nurse Daisy has issued instructions.'

'I couldn't wear anything like that, you know. It wouldn't suit me.' Elizabeth tried at once to evade the implication of that remark, not only because it so obviously proclaimed her high opinion of herself but also because it equally obviously underlined Alice's servile heredity. 'No, I wasn't thinking. You're doing something different.'

'I nursed my mother for six months. You learn things that way.'

'Oh, yes. Sorry.' Alice's severe tone upset her. 'No, I was meaning... I was meaning about passion.'

'What about passion?'

'I think I'd know if he had passion. You'd know, wouldn't you?'

Alice couldn't help smiling. She felt sure the young doctor had passion.

'Are you passionate about *him*?'

The girl blushed. 'I'm not saying.'

It was a nice way of puncturing Elizabeth's inflated sense of her new, uniquely important emotion. She flaunted her love for Gary Edstrom and gave herself airs as his personal assistant. Alice, meanwhile, kept her own secret to herself, aware how keen her feeling had been whenever the young Dr Simmons had been close to her in her mother's sickroom or downstairs in the drawing room or by the front door, though she had never dared use his forename aloud within earshot of the servants or the night nurse. Yet passion had filled the air as loudly as the insistent ticking of the grandfather clock in the hallway whose chiming could be heard throughout the house. So it amazed her how open Elizabeth could be about her love, how innocently unaware she was of the likely pain love could bring when unacknowledged, hidden, literally imprisoned by social custom and the shackles of politeness.

For Alice, though, the Mission had suddenly and quite unexpectedly brought a surprising emotional freedom. It might appear to be a kind of imprisonment, locked away as she had been in nursing duties under Nurse Daisy's instructions, but now she had her own *him*, her own secret love, as she dared to imagine it, because whenever *he* was there in the ward, or they smiled casually, or spoke casually, she felt her heart race with excitement. Dr Leo excited her. She had watched daily as he dealt with the incoming wounded and grew respectful of his careful, efficient manner. A bond had been created that was renewed daily by the nursing routine, including the smells of the job, into which she found herself being initiated slowly and painstakingly by a Nurse Daisy who recognised well enough what was happening.

Pugnacity may have been Nurse Daisy's public face. All her life, she was used to saying, she had fought. Right through a Californian girlhood, right through a stepfather's abuse and a violent marriage, right through her years of nursing in San Francisco and her missionary work overseas. She had grown tough. No one dared challenge her, disobey her, curry favour. When she gave an order, she expected it to be obeyed to the letter. She always worked briskly. Try as she might in the following weeks, Alice could never match Nurse Daisy's nimble dexterity in cleaning wounds, applying bandages, changing bed linen and making sheets fly up like sails before expertly flicking them beneath straw mattresses and tucking them into place.

What Alice soon also learned was that, for all her professional sharpness, Nurse Daisy's charitable heart showed itself in her round, very young-looking, almost girlishly innocent eyes. Emotional commitment on a personal level was another matter. The transient world of the Chinese and Russian sick in such a charity ward suited her. She did not need to be involved. She openly admitted she was Christian, sure, but she did not proselytise for the Mission. She just did what she had to do, as she put it. Yet she liked talking. She talked freely to her locally recruited nurses, giving them names like Lulu, Dolly, Sally, Molly. She also insisted they hid their black hair beneath the starched, winged headdresses. They would bow and smile politely and perhaps enjoy being talked to and given new names. Whether or not they really understood, Alice doubted. Nurse Daisy only spoke English, but they liked being trained, having roles and responsibilities and working to the strict patterns laid down by her. But they were never confided in. Confidences were for Dr Francis Rawls.

He was bespectacled, quiet-spoken, the very opposite in many ways. In fact, as Alice soon discovered, there was nothing more between them than a professional devotion to the healing art. Small, neat, slim, even dapper, sometimes from the back almost indistinguishable from his Chinese co-workers and assistants, he was inclined to be fussy and indecisive. These were qualities that obviously appealed to the most vulnerable parts of Nurse Daisy's nature. She lavished on him as much care and attention as she would have given to an adored father. Some ten years her senior, he did not ignore her feeling for him so much as remain impregnably unaffected by it and frankly preferred the company of the Chinese assistants, who reciprocated by doting on him as their friend and teacher.

Neither Nurse Daisy nor Dr Rawls knew much Russian, but it was the language spoken among all new patients in the ground-floor ward. Alice was drawn to it as she was drawn to Leo Nikitin. She felt the elaborately ornate alphabet seen for the first time in the names of stations on the train journey across Russia matched imperfectly the soft, alluring, intriguing, percussive resonance of a language sounding as mysterious as the murmurs in seashells she had listened to on seaside holidays as a child, but she wished to know it, its sibilant richness, its exuberance and expressiveness, the lilt of it when Leo recited Pushkin's poetry in his deep voice. It seemed to banish what struck her now as so small about her previous life. She had lived in a slot, in the to-and-fro of seeing to her mother's needs, of busying herself day after day with the routines of the London household, of knowing her mother was slowly dying.

'Your father,' Leo asked, 'what did he do?'

'He ran the New York office. Mr Wyburn, Leonard Wyburn, he ran the office in London. My father used to come to London regularly perhaps six, seven times a year, mostly to meet partners at Lloyd's. He'd stay for a while, then go back, but my mother, she preferred to live in London.'

'Why?'

'He had a mistress, that's why.'

The line of his eyebrows lifted intelligently as he nodded. 'And you were expected to...'

'Oh, yes. To keep quiet. Yes, that was expected of me.'

'You were not angry?'

'With my father? No, not really. My mother demanded a lot. She was not an easy person. I loved her, you see. We were very close. At the end, though...'

She raised her eyes to his in the certainty that he would understand. The memory of it made her stare a moment, as if she were at the bedside again, not in the quietness of the small Mission dining room with vehicles and people visible outside.

'I see.'

'The house in London is still being kept open.' Her fingers round a half-finished mug of coffee, she said it dreamily, not even daring to recall what the recent past had been like. 'I left it in rather a mess because my father said, would I, you know, come with them, Elizabeth and Oliver? After all, I'd been a governess before that. For a while. Anyhow I agreed, not really knowing what it would be like. Their uncle… Well, we didn't know he was ill.'

'Nurse Daisy calls you American Alice. New York is your home?'

'Oh, yes, I'm on my way home. Via China.' She laughed. 'That sounds silly, doesn't it?'

He pursed his lips before allowing them to form a smile and drummed his fingers lightly on the table. Whether he was really amused, she had no idea. Perhaps he was embarrassed. Suddenly he brought out a watch from a waistcoat pocket, looked at it and excused himself. The briskness of his action suggested indifference. Despite knowing she should follow his example, she stayed where she was and stared out of the window at the roadway. If she had had the will power, she often told herself at night, she would have got the safe conduct by hook or by crook and gone to Tokyo and San Francisco and said dammit, I'm free! After all, she had done what her father asked and her father would send her money. Shouldn't she go? What was keeping her?

A residue of past anxieties, chimeras swelling at night into giant icebergs of apprehension that broke any notion of self-assertion into fragments, made her certain she could not go back. Not at least to the old London life. The counterbalancing dangers of the Mission, recruitment to Nurse Daisy's routines, even Leo Nikitin's likely indifference had a kind of novelty appeal. She could float now, she thought, not have to make decisions day after day. She could lie awake in a sea of darkness and let Leo Nikitin's features float towards her and be content with his indifference. It pleased her to think she could challenge it.

Two nights later she sat bolt upright in bed and listened. There was a distant tapping sound. Assuming it was footsteps or the banging of shutters, she lay back, but after a moment or so the sound identified itself more clearly as a soft bell-like ringing accompanied by a man's voice. Equally softly a door banged. The voice and the ringing could be heard again. She crept out of bed without waking Elizabeth in the adjoining bed.

Strong gusts of the newly risen wind made the whole house creak enough to drown what she was doing as she pulled on her slippers and her old coat and peered into the hallway. Light coming from a bedroom doorway down the passage enlarged and lessened as the door moved to and fro in the wind. It was Uncle Elliott's room. Access to it was always strictly limited on Vassia's orders and the door was rarely open. She tiptoed towards it. A nightlight glowing inside revealed a Chinese nurse fast asleep in a chair and the old man struggling to reach a bottle on a side-table. He was tapping it with a teaspoon. She fastened the door behind her as she stepped into the room. He blinked rapidly, evidently trying to focus.

'Ah, Alice, my dear…' He indicated that he would like her to recover his pince-nez from the floor. 'Thank you, thank you.'

Only a small dose was to be taken from the bottle but his hand shook so much she administered the required amount herself. He smiled at her and lay back against pillows piled up against the bed-head.

She knew she had intruded and was about to return to her room when, fastening the pince-nez on the bridge of his nose, he made a little beckoning movement towards a chair beside his bed. Though the room was as warm as ever from a stove shedding an orange glow on to the carpeted floor, she pulled her old coat tightly round her as she sat down. The whine of the wind in the stove chimney seemed to bring the icy night right into the room. She was as embarrassed by the mess her hair was in as by uncertainty about whether he was really aware of her, since the light from the stove turned his features into a mask pierced by two round orange flames flickering in the lenses of the pince-nez. She pretended to busy herself with fixing her hair but could not fail to glimpse her surroundings, the room's dark privacy, its holiness as a sanctum and her own role as an intruder suddenly given access to the old man's whole life laid bare in the ghostly photographs and the shelves of books.

'Stay. Please.'

'Wouldn't it be better if I... You'd want to sleep now, wouldn't you?'

'No, no.'

He apologised for having woken her. Patting her hair into place, she leaned forward to listen to words emerging slowly and softly out of his mask of a face. He said how glad he was she had decided to stay.

'We need you, you know. I am afraid they have become very sensitive, very...'

'Who?'

'... very nervous. After such defeats. The Russian authorities.'

'Oh.'

'You are coming from England. To them it means...' She waited a perceptible moment for the sentence to be completed. 'You are an enemy is what it means. A spy.'

'Gary Edstrom – sorry, sir, I mean the Reverend Gary... he told us.'

He raised a finger to his lips. 'Not too loud.' A nod towards the Chinese nurse. 'Poor woman, she deserves to sleep. So Gary told you – good. We have to be neutral. I have always insisted. But because of me, you're an enemy, a spy. And the children... I had hoped...'

She anticipated what he wanted to say, but the way he paused and began fingering the bedclothes at chest height reminded her of what her mother had done so frequently before the end. Clasping her hands tightly, she sighed and looked down at the floor.

'Of course, I think I know...'

'It is Oliver, the boy, he worries me. He is so like my brother Leonard, so like him at that age. I could hardly believe it when I saw him. He's like him in other ways, too.'

She had known Oliver only slightly before accompanying him on the rail journey. It had brought them very close together emotionally, to the point when she could even think of him as a younger brother. Callow and still a child, he was clever and charming, but essentially a loner. He wanted to be treated as a grown-up and she respected him for insisting on living apart since arriving in the Mission.

'He is a determined boy, quite determined in his own mind. He shows such *determination*. Leonard was like that. Where did Oliver go to school?'

'I think he had tutors.'

'No proper school, then?'

'He went to one school, I think, and then said he preferred not to go back. I'll ask him tomorrow.'

'No, no. I'm asking because when we had a chance of talking a couple of nights ago, he wouldn't say anything about his schooling. He just told me he wanted to be a soldier. Preferred not to go back indeed!' The old man chuckled quietly. 'Just like Leonard! I am sorry about his accommodation, you know. We closed the houses when the others left. That attic place was all we had. He's a good boy. He is working for Mr Wei. You know Mr Wei?'

'Oh, yes.'

'In the library. That's where he's working.' The old man yawned. 'It'll keep him from being a soldier, that's for sure! But he is very determined to do something special. Poor boy, we were all like that at that age. Look after him, my dear, will you. He will be our future, you know.'

'I will try, of course.'

'Look after him.'

He said nothing after that. His white head of hair, the curly eyebrows and the wrinkled features, like the fingers resting on the bedclothes, were so still at that moment she could not help thinking of him as the very image of an Old Testament prophet, perhaps an oddly clerkish or schoolmasterly Moses wearing pince-nez propped at a slight angle. Feeling certain he must have fallen asleep, she stood up as quietly as possible and made for the door.

'You will also.'

The words spoken to her back were so startling she thought there was someone else in the room.

'Pardon?'

'You will, my dear.'

She glanced round in a panic and saw he was now looking at her directly, smiling, holding out his hand, even giving the impression of forcing an intimacy on her by the way his fingers reached out and grasped hers so firmly.

She found herself sitting down again.

'You will do something great, my dear,' he said softly.

For some reason she felt short of breath as he spoke, as if the room had suddenly become devoid of all breathable air and had grown noticeably colder. The shock of hearing him speak rather than what he said made her begin to tremble.

'I am telling you this because I have a modest gift of prophecy. Believe me. You will, you *will* do something... something great! But you also know how difficult your life might be, don't you? You're called American Alice, aren't you, but being American is ethnically such a mixture. I mean a handsome woman like you, my dear, coloured, as they call it, but so English in many ways, well, you know how people think. Be bold!'

The grip on her fingers remained firm. She could do nothing but stare back at the eyes faintly glistening behind the orange flicker in the lenses. There was no resisting the firm grip.

'I know.'

All she could do was gulp and try hard to fill her lungs with air. The grip he exerted was just like the sense of being caught here in the Mission, held by it, stuck in it, and yet it was also a grip acknowledging his love.

Suddenly a longstanding inhibition loosened inside her and seemed to set her free.

'I know. As a girl I knew it. I told myself I couldn't change. My great-grandmother had been black – oh, yes, a handsome black woman who married her white master and had children... That's my heritage. It's a mixture, as you say. Indian maybe at the start, so my mother maintained, then white, then black, then white again, then coloured, that's how I'm American, that's what star-spangled means. And I'm proud to be that, you know. So thank you, I'll be bold.'

The words came from her of their own accord, she could not tell how, and she felt silly thanking him for her own determination to be bold, but the words had the effect of letting him relax his grip. Slowly his fingers slipped away from hers. It struck her that there was a slight smile creasing his lips as he seemed to drift away from her into the contentment of a deep sleep.

She did not move immediately. Still trembling, she never felt less like a heroine. All she knew was that she would look after Oliver as best she could, no matter how determined he was. That would be boldness of a sort and a lot easier than trying to enact some role bestowed on her by the old man now apparently asleep beside her. In any case, reflecting on it made her tired. She closed her eyes. Reddish underwater blooms pressed against the insides of her eyelids and reminded her, as if in pity for her past and future self, of the nightly vigils spent at her mother's bedside and the ever-present need to nurse the wounded as well as the now added need to achieve some purpose way beyond her imagining.

Suddenly the outside world intruded. Molten stripes burned their way into her eyes and she opened them wide to see a brilliant white light shine through the slits in the shutters. Explosions broke out in the distance. Dogs began barking somewhere among the houses. The Chinese woman awoke, they stared at each other like ghosts in the returning glow of the nightlight and then little shooing motions persuaded Alice to leave.

She sprang to her feet. Vassia appeared in the doorway. He rushed past her and anxiously bent over the bed.

5

Water buckets being lifted from the well, men running yoked across the yard and other hurrying feet as 'honey buckets' were carried off on handcarts filled the dusk with an uneasy, echoing clamour. She was about to go to the dining room for supper when Nurse Daisy told her Mr Wei wanted to see her and she found him in the Mission entrance with a young Chinese man whom he introduced as his son-in-law.

'My daughter - very much needing you, Miss Alice. Her boy - sick, very sick. You are angel, Miss Alice. Please.'

He pointed to his throat.

She had no idea what he meant, so surprised and puzzled was she to be called an angel. Mr Wei smiled, bowed, mentioned some name she did not catch and insisted she hurry, hurry, because the curfew was imminent. A small rickshaw-type vehicle was waiting for her. She was strapped into the seat with a warm cover drawn over her and the son-in-law took his place in the shafts and began running.

To cries of 'Hurry! Hurry!' she was pulled away at once and all she could see was a hat with earflaps bobbing up and down above the level of the front leather apron and tasselled fringe of the roof overhang. In this way she was swayed and jerked over cobblestones, through the eastern gate and along streets mostly visible as little more than silhouetted rooftops. It was exhilarating and enjoyable after a fashion. She could see why Chinese ladies enjoyed this mode of travel. Except that she had not tell where she was going, or why, and the wind, inescapable at the best of times, came bitingly into the vehicle's interior once they passed through the western gate and began a shaking, shivering progress down rutted lanes through low-roofed houses dark as tombstones in the evening twilight. Despite her nurse's uniform, her frilly bonnet and the warm cover she shivered and pushed her hands into the opposing starched cuffs of her sleeves to protect them from the cold, but more shocking even than the cold or the jerky ride was the sudden loud wail of a locomotive nearby.

It was such an unusual sound. Within a minute or so she glimpsed jets of white steam rising above the black lines of telegraph wires and knew the station must be close.

They halted suddenly. The apron was unfixed and the son-in-law, evidently out of breath, bowed politely. She stepped out and was quickly guided over debris of what may once have been carefully laid wooden sleepers but had become a series of crevices and ruts now slippery with ice. Unsteady underfoot, her nerves became unsteady as well. A wave of mistrust spilled over her. Could she trust this son-in-law? What was she doing here anyhow? A high fence, the wind making the matting flap, a gate banging, then a figure bending towards her in the half-light of a lantern and shadows leaping this way and that. She should run, run away, she thought. Lifted towards her with a gleam of eyes was a face, yellow, masculine, wizened and expectant enough to convince her to follow the lantern light for want of any other choice up a brick path towards a doorway, which she did, holding on to her bonnet, more or less certain of coming peril and confounded by the incomprehensibility of Chinese words exchanged in the darkness amid madly blowing chimney smoke from a shuttered house.

The next instant there was a flash of light. She almost fell back. The door had opened, bamboo drapes clattered together and she was led into an interior so bright she had to shield her eyes.

'Ah, so glad!'

It was Leo who spoke. She stared at him with her mouth ridiculously open in astonishment. It came to her then that this was the name Mr Wei had mentioned and she should have been aware of it from the start and therefore not been anxious.

'You did not know?'

'No, I…' She explained what had confused her. He nodded and then swept an arm round in a kind of vague introduction. Five people bowed towards her in the wake of the gesture, the man with the wizened face still holding the lantern, a very elderly Chinese man who rose briefly from his seat by a small table, a long-stemmed pipe in one hand, an elderly woman in the act of pouring water into a bowl, a much younger woman and the son-in-law, now bare-headed, his black hair matted thickly across his forehead. All were impassive, yellow, unblinking. Leo introduced her.

'Miss May, Alice.'

The words provoked a wave of spontaneous bows, though she knew they had not understood. His own immediate action, disregarding all etiquette, it seemed, was to come quickly towards her. She noticed there were little beads of sweat on his forehead and eyebrows, but, perhaps rudely, she raised her hand to cover her nose and mouth against the bad odour of tobacco and cooking smells that permeated the atmosphere. His expression flickered between uncertainty and hurt at what looked like a gesture of rejection.

'Please, I must explain. You see...'

She dispersed niceties by insisting on her forename.

'Please call me Alice. Tell me why I'm here.'

'Yes. I must tell you. Alice. Please let me...'

He smiled as he spoke her name and took the liberty of seizing her hand. The action puzzled her and even seemed too familiar. She flinched slightly, until he asked if he could please see her fingers.

'My fingers?'

'Please.'

'Nurse Daisy insisted, you know...'

'Insisted?'

'We keep our nails cut.'

'Ah, I see. But...'

If her fingers were as slim as he thought they were, she would be able to save a life, he whispered.

The softly spoken words caught everyone's attention and brought silence. Even the pouring of the water stopped and the wind's noise lessened. It did not alter the sense, which wrapped itself round her like the room's smell, that she was resented, as Leo was resented, and it would take very little for the hostility in the room to show itself. The instant, though, his fingers touched hers, they conveyed a reassuring warmth and confidence.

'Little boy...'

'Oh, Mr Wei said, yes...'

'Very sick.'

Leo glanced towards a corner of the room. At first she could not be sure what he meant, until she noticed a hoarse sound and saw that the young woman had knelt down beside a small bench. Lying on the bench on some matting was a small figure that she recognised as a boy of about four or five in a dirty nightshirt with bare legs. His narrow rib cage quivered each time he attempted to draw breath and a laboured, painful wheezing accompanied by coughing and grunting now seemed to fill the room.

More alarming was the way the boy's frightened, feverishly bright almond eyes turned a despairing stare towards her as she turned to look at him. They seemed to stick knives into her heart out of a small yellow face so bluish and sickly it looked more like a tiny old man's than a boy's. She glanced away almost at once.

'Trach-e-ot-omy,' Leo whispered, still holding her fingers.

She did not know what he was talking about. 'Tracky what?'

'Croup. You call it, yes?'

'Croup, yes.'

'Very sick, you can see. You can save him. Let me see, please.' He studied her fingers carefully, particularly the two rings. 'Will you help?'

'Will I?'

'Will you save his life?'

'How?'

He explained that the boy should be in hospital for a tracheotomy, but there was apparently a fear of hospitals, particularly a fear of surgery.

'Simple people, you see.'

She looked round at the watching faces. It occurred to her for the first time that poverty as well as resentment and mistrust showed in their watchfulness.

'No, no,' he said, 'no surgery. So instead...'

A narrow curved metal tube with a round enlargement at one end appeared in his hand. It was shiny and clinical and looked vaguely like some kind of weapon.

'I have tried to use this to help him... help him to breathe. It must go in trachea.'

'What is it?'

'It is new, American. Mister O'Dwyer, he made it. You put it in.... Look, I show you.'

He showed her a little printed diagram of what was called *The O'Dwyer Patent Intubator.* She saw the instructions were in English, which was a relief, with signs pointing to *larynx*, *epiglottis* and *trachea* in a poorly drawn cross section of a human throat. Arrows indicated how the instrument was to be correctly inserted into a supine human figure that looked remarkably lifeless.

Leo went on whispering. 'In your left hand you... Look, it shows you. You use your finger and O'Dwyer tube, it goes into trachea. It stays. He can breathe.'

She stared at the instructions and then raised her eyes.

'What's that do?'

'Saves his life.'

'Saves his life?'

He gave a nod. 'I try...my fingers are too big.' Leo pointed at the boy. 'I try but...'

She studied Leo's face a moment and saw the anxiety and knew she would do anything at that moment to please him. It would help him to salvage some self-respect, for one thing, since she now grasped why the audience was apparently so hostile. He had failed and was now relying on her. It showed that he *did* care.

More than that, she would do it for herself, to prove she could, bravado or not. She blinked hard, took a long further look at the diagram, nodded and licked her lips.

'Yes, I will try.'

The instant he told her to remove her rings and wash her hands, her fears returned. She ought not to attempt anything so risky, so untried, so new. But she plunged her hands in the bowl of water and felt determined not to give up.

She was more certain still when she turned back towards the bench and saw the boy's eyes again fixed on her as he tried to breathe. For several seconds there was nothing to be heard above his painful gasping except the distant wail of a locomotive. Even Leo's voice giving instructions seemed remote, as if in another room, because she was so concentrated on the boy.

He knew what was going to happen next because it had happened before. The torture would be repeated. He thrashed about in a feeble way and squirmed but the attempt to breathe, the short desperate gasps and grunts, left him open-mouthed and his eyes bulging. Then he suddenly gave up the struggle. He fought for breath. The young woman kneeling on the other side of the bench whispered soothing words.

Alice sank on to her knees beside Leo. He pointed into the boy's mouth and held up the diagram so she could see it clearly.

'There, see – epi-glottis.'

He signed for more light and the wizened man with the lantern leant over them.

'Left finger, yes, yes, that's right – try to press epi-glott-is… forward, forward.'

Press it forward, Alice told herself. She looked round at Leo. It amazed her to see over his shoulder more faces, this time the faces of children.

'Then slide in tube… with guide…'

Slide in the tube with the guide, she told herself.

'Remove guide when tube is in… See, it says so.'

The boy's eyes continued bulging despite the bright light of two lanterns. She inserted her left index finger into his mouth and could feel something small and soft jumping and throbbing under her touch. The tube with its guide and handle was in her right hand. Trying to do as she had been told, she pushed the tube down the length of her left index finger. It seemed to go a short way and then meet resistance. The boy gagged and tried to pull away, but was held back.

Leo restrained her. She saw the mother's eyes opposite were burning with hurt and suspicion. At once she withdrew the tube, feeling bullied and harassed.

The boy coughed painfully, squirmed with pain, started crying, teardrops ran down the sides of his face and the hoarse grunting was renewed.

'Again,' said Leo softly.

She took the intubator again and this time fumbled with it in the boy's throat, which was messy and made her feel disgusted. After a while, somewhat to her disbelief, it found its way in and she began removing the guide.

Practically at once, breathless, his face contracting in pain, the boy spat the tube out along with drops of bloody saliva. The mother groaned loudly. An echoing wail filled the room.

'I can't!' Alice cried. She felt she would break down in tears.

Leo disregarded this, wiped the intubator and handed it back to her.

'Again,' was all he whispered. 'Please.'

Resentfully she seized the instrument of torture. His very calmness did not reassure her so much as pose a challenge. She would show him, she thought. She would show them all. This time, following the diagram, she shifted to the end of the bench, so that the crown of the boy's head was facing her, took in a deep breath and felt as carefully as she could for the larynx. It had swelled and was more difficult to keep still. She muttered a small prayer.

The boy squirmed and fought, his mouth all sticky from her touch, and tried to squeal, but was again held down. She introduced the tube again along her finger. For an instant, which seemed as long as half a minute, the protuberant eyes opened wide in horror and the small body went rigid.

I have killed him, she thought. Shutting her eyes, she let go of the instrument and tried to rise. The kneeling had made her stiff. She couldn't. She dared not move, dared not open her eyes to face the Chinese, especially the mother who knelt opposite her. She was certain she had killed the boy. She had tried and failed like Leo. So-called superior Western medical knowledge could only do one thing – *kill children!* She clasped her fingers together, still slimy and sticky, and made an effort to pray for what she hoped would be forgiveness.

A moment later something happened. Leo was leaning over her. Startled by the closeness of his body from which she caught a whiff of his sweat, she opened her eyes, looked down and saw the boy lying there stock still with the handle sticking out of his mouth. She was sure he was dead, but to her surprise Leo seemed very calm. He gently removed the guide.

The noise of shunted wagons filled the room. They were like discordant bells clanging loudly on a gradually descending scale and finally dying away into silence. It terrified her how the silence re-entered the room from the cold outside and froze them all into a motionless expectancy. She looked round in fright. The leaning faces were all fixed on the boy, quite expressionless in the bland, gold radiance of the lanterns.

Suddenly she felt lips on her cheek.

'You've done it,' Leo whispered

The boy was breathing quietly. The mother was wiping away tears and mucous. Her face, lifted to Alice's, was plain, workaday and solemn, but a light of relief glowed in her tired eyes and she bowed her head slightly in acknowledgement of the relief brought to her son. Then Alice found herself lifted up. Leo had pulled her gently to her feet and was hugging her. In relief and gratitude she let his arms press her against him. There was no embarrassment, none except his warmth gradually enfolding her, so that all she noted as she looked over his shoulder was the children making noises and being hushed and the adults beginning to talk softly.

It was exactly what she wanted – to be clasped and appreciated and given renewal of strength. She had scarcely realized how exhausted she was.

'Alice, my dear,' he whispered, 'thank you, thank you. He will be better now. Mr Wei promised to send angel…'

'Mr Wei!' She laughed weakly. 'Oh, he called me an angel! Well, if I've helped to save his grandson…'

'No, no, he is not.'

'Not?'

The relationship was somehow blighted by disgrace. Alice never discovered whether the boy was illegitimate or exactly why Mr Wei's daughter and son-in-law lived in such relative poverty. She discovered only that Leo was always ready to help in any circumstances but rarely prepared to talk about it. It was also the first time she had come face to face with ordinary Chinese. Forced upon her now was her own life, lived so long in security and comfort, cosseted, she had to admit, from precisely what she saw in the faces looking at her in the lantern light. Instead of humility towards them or respect or pity, she was aware only of the mutual simplicity of feeling that they showed in bowing to her and she reciprocated in bowing back as if they were simply waving to each other from different banks of an unbridgeable river.

'So now we go home,' said Leo, lowering his arms.

***

The feel of the boy's mouth and throat, the very smallness, the touch-and-go of inserting the intubator tended to haunt her thoughts as the memory returned again and again. Oh, she was an angel, sure, and had done what the old man predicted! That much was a comforting support against the remnants of the experience. It made her happy to let the carriage rock her to and fro in silence as she and Leo returned to the Mission that night, but the rings on her fingers were a constant reminder of the feel of mucous, of something too soft, too indefinable, so that she almost forgot Leo had kissed and hugged her and was amazed when, after alighting from the carriage in the Mission entrance, he suddenly kissed her again on both cheeks and made the sign of the cross over her.

'Thank you, thank you, thank you.'

The words were there on the air, offered to her as he bowed and gave little shakes of his head in demonstration of his gratitude, but as before in her life she felt uncertain of the fondness. Should she snatch the words out of the air and believe them to mean something more? She questioned herself, doubtful as ever, more than ever conscious that there was some skein of servility binding her to a subordinate condition of mind as well as feeling. So she spoke to no one and did not even share her thoughts with Elizabeth. The next day, what is more, Dr Leo Nikitin appeared to have left the Mission. The news was deeply bewildering and hurtful. 'On Russian business,' so Nurse Daisy said. Why 'on Russian business'? What sort of business could that be? But Nurse Daisy did not know, nor did she know when he would be back.

The news left Alice worried and subject to fits of annoyance, despair and tearfulness. After all, he surely owed her something; or had he absented himself because he hadn't the courage to thank her or maybe didn't want to see her again? The absence did nothing to ennoble her feelings for him, nor did it lessen her own doubts about herself. Had his kisses and his gratitude meant nothing at all? Circumstances, though, the war, that was the problem. It was the war, everybody said. She could hardly overlook the fact that all round her so much was being attributed to the war and its uncertainties.

'American Alice! American Alice!'

She had slept poorly that night and here was Nurse Daisy calling out the next morning. An invitation had arrived.

'What?'

'Here! It's addressed to you, Miss Alice May. Don't you recognise the handwriting? I guess you'd best put on your best dress and maybe deck yourself out a bit.'

The invitation inside the handwritten envelope was copperplate and formal. It announced that a private room had been booked that evening at a local Chinese restaurant and Dr Leo Nikitin 'will greatly appreciate the attendance of Miss Alice May'.

Nurse Daisy's advice was timely, sure, but Alice's best dress was her *blue* dress, the only one she had brought with her in the belief that there would only be a short stopover in China. Elizabeth helped her with some of her face powder and *eau de cologne*, perfumes that built a kind of tent round her, along with the loan of some jewellery. Mr Wei also helped her. He showed her the way to the restaurant, anxious as he did so to offer his thanks for helping his daughter's boy to get well and with the help of such gratitude letting her calm her nerves.

Bowing very low to her at the restaurant's entrance, he wished her happiness. For her part, she entered the place keenly aware of stares from other diners, but, being quickly escorted to a private room, felt even more self-conscious to find it cramped and rather airless and dominated by an over-bright glitter of long-stemmed candles in cut-glass candelabra. A round table and three high-backed chairs all presented themselves to her twice over through being repeated dully in a wall mirror draped with silk hangings. It looked like a window on to a strange little cupboard in which she was surprised to be standing.

The room was less odd than Leo's welcome. He appeared awkward and shy in rising at her entrance, smiling a trifle too stiffly and rather awkwardly kissing her hand, only to suddenly break off his greetings to introduce someone who came in just behind her. She was astonished to find there was a quite unexpected further guest.

'Takeo-san, Miss May, Alice, if I may… Here is my good friend, Takeo-san. He is Yellow Peril.'

'Yellow Pellil, yes. I am Yellow Pellil, honolable lady. Pleased to meet you.'

The small man, dressed in a dark suit with a jacket so tightly buttoned it made him look like a toy soldier, bowed smartly and smiled with a sort of childlike amusement at being introduced as 'Yellow Peril'. Alice had seen him often in the hospital wing, sometimes indeed talking to Leo, but always dressed in the anonymous garments of the medical staff with a number on his back. She had assumed he was one of the Chinese assistants trained by Dr Rawls. Awkwardly she held out a hand and then withdrew it in embarrassment the moment he bowed a second time.

Confronting her there in the small room, they looked so utterly different. Leo's face was strong, square, with a prominent nose and sensitive, shapely mouth, his complexion burnished by the candlelight to a dark pink above a white dress shirt and loosely knotted necktie, while the Japanese face of his friend was so much smaller and more delicate with its light-ochre complexion and round spectacles that enlarged glistening elongated amber eyes. Both men smiled.

'I need to explain, *we* need to explain, I know, I know, but I wish to begin *po-russki* - with toast to my friends!' Leo had poured out small glasses of vodka that he now handed to his guests. 'Please!'

Takeo-san lifted the small glass in imitation of his host, looked slowly from Leo to Alice and with a slow, very considered movement tipped the glass into his mouth in a way that upended his spectacle lenses and made them glitter. Alice followed his example, gasped at the unaccustomed fieriness of the vodka, began coughing and was pleased to see both men smile back at her as she covered her mouth with a napkin. In no time she felt a glow of warmth spread through her.

Chinese servants rushed in with bowls of food and the meal started without any preliminaries. Takeo-san ate expertly with chopsticks and Leo with a spoon. Rice, pieces of chicken, pork in sweet-and-sour sauce, bean sprouts, tastes Alice had never encountered before, accompanied by sake wine of Takeo-san's choice, were a backdrop to her own happiness in receiving such a treat. She surprised herself by glowing in front of the two men, conscious how her eyes shone, how she had acquired an unusual power to attract or subordinate with a glance or a word or a smile. Above all, she recognised she was being privileged by Leo's close attention.

'I wish to say I owe Miss May – Alice - many, many thanks. You see without Alice.' he told his friend, 'I could not save boy's life. And I also must explain I have been away – I must say *why* I have been away – and we, Takeo-san and I, we must explain *why* we must… *why* we must be here today.'

'Good. Velly good,' said the Japanese.

'First of all about boy,' said Leo.

'It is very good news, I know,' said Alice. 'Mr Wei told me.'

'Yes, he is recovering.'

'Suppose you will always…be…nurse, yes?' Takeo-san asked very politely.

'I nursed my mother, that's all. My fingers are small, that's how I was able to help the boy.'

'Your rings,' asked Leo, 'on your fingers… you take them off… what are they?'

She explained that one ring, a slim gold band, had belonged to her mother. The other was silver in the shape of a small turtle. It struck her suddenly that his interest in her rings might be because they indicated some attachment.

'Turt-le? Why? What is it?'

'What's a turtle?'

'Yes, turt-le, what is it?'

'I suppose it's like a large tortoise.'

'Tortoise! Oh, yes.'

'It doesn't mean I'm engaged or anything. Before my mother fell ill I taught two girls. They were very fond of me. They used to joke that another Alice, the Alice of *Alice in Wonderland* and her friends had called Lewis Carroll, their teacher, Tortoise because he "taught us". They couldn't call me Tortoise, instead they called me Turtle. I didn't mind. They gave me this ring when they left.'

'So it is not sign of... no?'

'No, no.' She was amused by the look of relief on his face.

He cleared his throat. 'They left, you say?'

'They went off to India. Their father was in the civil service.'

'India is Blitish empire, yes?' asked Takeo-san.

'India is, yes.'

There were awkwardnesses, the conversation trickled from one question to another and in its slow way the meal progressed through unusual tastes and sips of wine until Alice felt that common ground had been established between all three. She could sense that Leo and Takeo-san had been accustomed to each other's company for long enough to ensure a mutual confidence. The laughter, the smiles, even the compliments seemed genuinely spontaneous. Until the tone of the occasion changed when Takeo-san posed a question so politely she did not immediately realize what it meant.

'You like plivate life, honolable lady?'

Private life! She had never been asked such a thing before! The amber eyes behind the enlarging lenses were gazing at her with apparent seriousness.

'Private life? Yes, of course.'

'What does it mean?'

'Takeo-san is right, you know. I always wonder, too. Private – what does it mean?' Leo was twisting the stem of his wineglass between finger and thumb as he spoke. '*Priv-ate* – what is it?'

'It's just, you know...' She did not know what to say.

'And,' he went on, 'you have *private* life. We like *private* life, Takeo-san and I. But...but...'

'But what?'

He looked straight at her and smiled. 'It is not possible. For us private life is not possible.'

He drank some of the wine. Wiping his mouth, he changed the subject by saying his friend wished to speak.

The Japanese sat very straight-backed. His bright amber eyes conveyed his embarrassment. Obviously trying to master his emotions, he pressed the palms of his hands together prayerfully.

'I wish to say, honolable lady, what Dr Leo must say.'

The meal was drawing to a close and she imagined Takeo-san was making a final speech.

'You must be his flend, Miss Alice.'

Uncertain what this could mean, she was reassured when Leo responded with a laugh. Takeo-san promptly turned to her and declared with great earnestness:

'I wish, honolable lady, to be plivate person. Forgive me if I am not speaking good English. You are plivate person and you know what it is when you are plivate person. In my countly we have spillit of loyalty. You know what it is – we must be loyal. Can you, honolable lady, be loyal person and plivate person?'

Her look of amazement deterred him for a moment. He drew his hands apart and appeared to raise them in a kind of blessing. His next words, though, astonished her.

'We call it *bushido*. You know what is it? *Bushido* is spillit of loyalty. Loyalty to countly, loyalty to law, loyalty to our Empellor. *Bushi* is best person in countly. We say "As chelly blossom among flowers, so is *bushi* among men."'

'I see.' She tried to show polite understanding and this seemed to please him.

'Yes, yes! In my countly *bushi,* they only serve. Velly unselfish.' He paused and brought the palms of his hands together once again. 'You unlerstand?'

'I think so.' She looked to Leo for guidance but he was staring up at the ceiling.

'So you see I must serve. I must be loyal servant of my countly.' Takeo-san rose slowly to his feet. 'Honolable lady, I know you are good person. I wish you happiness. I wish to say toast.'

He held up his glass for Leo to replenish it and then held the filled glass towards her.

'It is my hope… my hope one day we meet again. But now I must… I must leave. I must serve my countly. I must say goodbye. Much happiness, honolable lady! Much happiness!'

He downed his glassful as he had downed the first. Takeo-san bowed very elaborately first to her, then to Leo and quickly, his lid of hair swinging across his forehead in evident embarrassment, turned on his heel and left the room. Leo did not even wave or get to his feet. He slumped deeper in his chair and drank another glass before picking up a slice of cucumber and crunching it between his teeth.

'Loyalty! Yes, it is loyalty!' He looked solemnly and rather blearily at Alice and gave a loose hand-wave. 'You have your friend one moment and next moment he is your enemy. Not *nice*, Miss Maddocks used to say. So it is what our dinner is about, you see.'

'He is going back to Japan?'

As she asked the question, she caught sight of herself in the wall mirror and was astonished by the dark gleam of her cheeks, as if they had received a coat of polish, and the way her hair had been loosened. The moment she raised her hands to make adjustments, she knew how silly the question was.

Leo gave a snort. 'He must be loyal to his warlords. Just as I must be loyal.'

'You must be loyal!'

'Of course. It is what I wanted to say as well. We go, he to his side, I to my side. We must serve our different warlords. So, Alice, my dear, I go tomorrow.'

So that's what it was! She knew she had been caught off guard by the realization that this was intended as a farewell meal and could hardly stop tears springing to her eyes. He merely went on twiddling the stem of his glass.

'I was busy, you see, these last days – High Command, imperial orders and so on, and so on. Dr Rawls, he knows, your nurse, she knows. And now you know.'

'By going you mean…?'

'Field hospital is what I mean.' He twiddled the stem of the glass more vigorously backwards and forwards between forefinger and thumb. 'Will you wait, my dear Alice? Can you wait? Perhaps I cannot expect… Perhaps it is too much… too much to ask.'

He raised his eyes and she lowered her arms. 'Of course I'll wait.'

How long? How long? It was the instant maddening thought, instantly followed by the smoothing, obliterating knowledge that she could wait forever, so long as his eyes were there to see her and she could smile back at him.

'You will not go to New York?'

'No, I… Not until…'

'You will wait here?'

'I will wait here.'

'Then I will come back,' he said. The twiddling stopped. 'Because I am in love with you, American Alice.'

She stretched a hand across to touch his free hand.

6

She was too shaken by the fact that he said he loved her, and the hopes bursting into flame in her heart gave her such happiness she couldn't help herself from trembling as he kissed her goodbye beneath the entrance arch to the Mission once the meal was over.

Then came the gap.

Dr Leo Nikitin's absence left a gap.

For Dr Francis Rawls it meant he no longer had help with operations and so operations for the Russian wounded were abandoned.

For Nikki Kozlov, arriving daily to oversee the admission of the wounded and take names, it meant, in his oddly accented English, that he was 'very sorr-*ee*' but orders had to be obeyed and all surgeons were now needed in the field hospitals.

For Alice, hearing this, it meant mostly tears shed secretly at night, blurring her gaze at the ceiling where strips of light from the shutters occasionally made zebra patterns followed by a lion's roar of distant explosions. Elizabeth, asleep in the adjacent bed, seemed as unaware of it as she was unaware of Alice's love.

The shared regret at Leo's absence lessened the personal sadness. Nurse Daisy was sure he'd be back. 'Bad penny,' she announced once, laughing. She had been fond of Leo and respectful of his quiet, patient efficiency. So often relying now on Alice to discover what might be wrong with one of the wounded, she tended to forget herself and say almost automatically 'Dr Leo'd know, wouldn't he?', acknowledging that both missed him. The different reasons merely increased their respect for each other.

The work also left Alice little time to brood since she had to admit she enjoyed being needed in the ward. There were times when she could have done with less replacing of dressings, less feeding the worst injured, less trying to understand what was said with the aid of Leo's dictionary, less of the comradeship of the Chinese nurses, and yet the daily changes, the influx and despatch of wounded, the men's largely taciturn acceptance of treatment, all gave her a sense of something truly achieved, something truly valuable. She told no one about Uncle Elliott's prophecy. It simply made her smile when she thought about it.

Her father's correspondence urged her to join him in New York as soon as possible. He had arranged for a letter of credit drawn on a Shanghai bank to be negotiable at its branch in Shenyang-Mukden, if the branch were still open, but Alice's immediate reaction was to put it aside in the hope that the 'bad penny' would turn up. She had promised she would wait and she would keep her promise. The war wouldn't last long into the New Year, Nikki Kozlov assured her. The Japanese were bound to suffer a catastrophic defeat once the fresh troops arrived.

She had to content herself, not with this certainty, however little it might be shared among those she nursed, but with the certainty that Leo would come back because that was the secret she nursed in her love for him. She knew there were barriers of ignorance that could come between them the longer they were parted - her ignorance of him, for example, his of her, but that very ignorance bolstered her certainty, as if the Russian language itself, what Nurse Daisy called the 'lingo' and didn't want to learn, made her all the more anxious to speak it as a means of sustaining her love. Determined in this way to lessen the pain of Leo's absence, she threw herself day by day all the more keenly into her nursing work until she began to assume almost sole responsibility for the ground floor ward.

Suddenly something very extraordinary happened.

'See to that fellow, will you!' It was what Nurse Daisy said a few days later after blowing her nose. She waved casually towards the centre of the ward. 'He says he's from London. He speaks the lingo.'

It was hard to believe! Someone from London speaking the lingo! There he was, sitting in a wicker armchair by the stove in the centre of the ground-floor ward. At first Alice mistook him for a Chinese because he was wearing a quilted Chinese jacket and then she noticed the medal pinned to it and the wooden crutch set against the chair arm. Then she saw the stump.

Hidden by the neatly folded, safety-pinned cloth of Russian uniform trousers, his left leg had been amputated. She had seen other wounded with similar injuries and was not surprised. What surprised her was the young face. It was beautiful, a boy's face, with a light-olive complexion and a healthy pinkness in the cheeks and lips. Most striking were the round, deep-brown eyes, brilliant and moist and absorptive. They stared vulnerably up at her. She could not help feeling the childish hurt in them the moment she saw them beneath the raven-black straight hair brushed firmly forward into a fringe.

'*Skazhite pozhaluista, vy kto?* Who are you? Do you speak English?'

'Isaac King, ma'am. People call me Izzy.'

'Izzy! But why are you here now? If you're English, you shouldn't be in the Russian army…'

He screwed up his boyish face into a replica of disgust.

''Cos I'm not!'

No, he had no official documents, even if his only real passport was his cockney English improbably embellished with a Russian accent and as odd-sounding as his account of being born in Kiev, where he had lived till he was fifteen, and then being sent to join his uncle Joseph in Blackfriars, London, to work in the latter's tobacconist's shop. After four years he had returned to Kiev to see his mother, which is why he had ended up here in China.

'They nab me is wot they do, nab me in Kiev, an' say I gotta be in their bleedin' army, an' I'm brought out 'ere, I am, to bleedin' China and now look wot they done to me! Bleedin' ruined me, they 'ave!'

He was awaiting confirmation that he was Isaac King, not Abramovich. His uncle had apparently been responsible for arranging matters in London. An application had been lodged a year before but he was still under-age and needed sponsorship. Meanwhile, he had been at Sha Ho and received a shrapnel wound to his leg. He pointed to his amputation.

'So it's ruined me, ain't it? But I'm not blamin' the Japs. I blame the bleedin' Russian army. One thing you gotta 'ave, you know.'

'What?'

'Yer name. You gotta 'ave the right bleedin' name.'

'Why?'

'Name's who you are, ain't it? Wivout the right name you're dust'n'ashes. An' all I get is this piece o' tin!'

So he was 'dust and ashes' because the Russian authorities had refused to accept his new name and given him a medal for injury received in face of the enemy, 'a piece o' tin' he didn't want. He did not whine at such injustice; he stated his case with a sort of innocent outrage at the sheer stupidity of it all.

'You live in London?' he asked.

She told him she had looked after her mother there but had been born and brought up in New York.

'You a Yank, then?'

She sniffed a little haughtily. 'I am. You can call me that. I am really on my way to New York, as a matter of fact. My mother died.'

She did not know why she adopted such a mixture of aloofness and candour with this new arrival. It was refreshing to find someone she could talk to on almost equal terms. There was also a certain childish boastfulness in her attitude that she could remember displaying as a girl at school. 'But I'm stuck here now,' she added as if making amends.

'Sorry about your ma.'

'Thank you. Can I get you anything?'

This seemed to insult him. 'I can get what I want, you know. I've learned.'

He had learned, he said, to use his crutch and he didn't need to be treated as an invalid.

'But you, you *are* stuck, aren't you?'

'Yes, I said so.'

'You can't go out on your own, is what I mean. It's dangerous, isn't it? 'Cos I'm tellin' you, miss, it's very, very dangerous!'

The irises of Izzy's eyes had a warning glitter. He whispered the remark in the crowded ward because it was true that she and Elizabeth and Nurse Daisy had been warned not to go into the old city unaccompanied. Two Russian women had recently been stabbed in broad daylight and their bodies left in the street; others had received threats. Reprisals were talked about, but wiser counsels had left the Chinese authorities to do what they could to find the perpetrators. As most people suspected without need of proof, drunken or marauding Russian troops were very likely the real culprits since instances of rape, violence, looting and indiscipline had become increasingly common. So she had been confined to the Mission.

In Izzy she found a protector and fellow spirit in a relationship that gave rise to all sorts of curiosity among the Russian wounded, most of it rude and improper. She only realized through his tuition how he much she needed protecting from the insinuations of lewd questions and remarks that she had scarcely been aware of until then. He became her guide to swear words. In Leo's absence only the less seriously wounded were admitted to the ground floor ward and they were sometimes more vigorous in their attentions. Attempts to fondle her, for example, touch her bosom, seize her by the neck, even kiss her occurred more often. Izzy taught her to quell such advances with an abracadabra of Russian phrases. Her readiness to understand and use such terms quickly earned her the men's respect and obedience, so much so that she sometimes had to watch her tongue literally for fear that the crude ripostes might become such day-to-day usage she could be coarsening herself in their eyes.

His abilities as an interpreter as well as his injury and medal entitled him to stay in the Mission as long as he wished. Also, he handled his crutch so expertly he was trusted to make frequent visits to city markets to do 'business', as he put it. He could procure medical supplies, of which there was a thriving black market, and food and drink. Various Chinese traders of his acquaintance knew exactly how to circumvent official channels.

Through his help, and in his company, Alice obtained a fleece-lined, ankle-length leather coat at a very modest price. She also bought small presents to give at Christmas. With Izzy at her side she made several visits to such sites of interest as the old imperial palace and the Manchu tombs. He personified a kind of buoyancy that was a complete contrast to the routine pessimism of most wounded admitted to the ward. She could have been badly depressed by Leo's absence but sharing in Izzy's utter refusal to feel self-pity, let alone resignation, renewed her zest for life and made her anxious for his future, since she recognised he was sometimes in great pain.

All he asked for was help from no less a source than his own namesake. ''Is Royal Majesty, *King* Edward, 'e'll see me right!' The British sovereign would rescue him from all his present troubles.

As for his chances, he said he mustn't seem to be defeatist because suspicion governed Russian attitudes and he had to be *on their bleedin' side*. He *knew* them, after all. Far worse than the Japanese capturing Port Arthur or defeating the Russian armies in Manchuria was the defeatist notion that revolution would stab them in the back. 'It'll come, you can be sure it will!' he whispered. He tapped his nose and she laughed.

In his company Alice could overlook the way the smells of the ward lurked on her uniform just as she did not really know what he meant when he talked about revolution. If her mother had seen her as she was now, she would have scolded her for 'not caring' – *Honey, you're letting yourself down. Don't never let yourself down.* She was aware from day to day how the uniform itself saved her from thinking too much about either her appearance or such remote, to her, masculine matters as politics while reinforcing the fact that she had no real privacy, no space of her own, sharing the room with Elizabeth as she did. The only place she could find to be by herself even for brief periods was the small Mission chapel.

She loved to slip into one of its wooden pews whenever she could. The austere bare white walls and shining brass cross on the plain altar always restored her equilibrium and lifted her spirits after a morning's duty on the ward. It was a place of quiet despite the wind-shaken windows and the noise of vehicles rattling down the avenue to the bridge. It was the nearest thing to a private room she could find where she could re-assemble her sense of self. Prayer had assisted her so much throughout the time she had nursed her mother in what she now realized was true security and comfort, far from the threat of war. To be here now in the chapel was security of a sort where she could pray for Leo and his safekeeping with a sense that divine protection was as certain as the walls of the Mission. But even that security seemed at times unsure and unreal.

At night flares and searchlights and sudden thuds interrupted sleep and eruptions of shutter-striped, eerie brightness would fill the bedroom. From one day to the next there had been conflicting reports about more than a million Russian troops preparing to attack.

'It sounds so close,' Elizabeth whispered from her bed. 'Do you think it's started?'

'The fighting's meant to be ten miles away. The wind brings it close.'

Alice was only repeating what she had been told. The bedroom dark, despite being interrupted by war from time to time as if it were a symptom of the climate, offered the opportunity to whisper a thousand intimate things that could seem anonymous when uttered in the intervening moments of quiet.

'I'm sure you're happy now, aren't you?'

'Oh, I love him, yes!'

'I'm so happy for you.'

'I think he may ask me...'

'You think he'll ask you...'

'We can't really think of anything until the war's over.'

It was so practical and unreal Alice could hardly believe she was hearing it.

'Well, if you think you've found him, someone, you know, who...'

'Yes,' came the answering whisper, 'I think so.'

'I'm sure you'll be happy.'

A moment later there was a feather-light touch on Alice's face. It was Elizabeth's hair. She had leaned across from her bed and was kissing her.

'Alice, dear, I love you. I really do. Yes, I'm sure I've found him. I'm sure, you know, he'll... Oh, I love the whole world! I love everyone in the world!'

*

In the first weeks of the New Year 1905 the world changed. Bits seemed to drift apart from Alice's life and leave all her relationships and hopes scattered and inconclusive. The same occurred in the ward. Overnight the Russian wounded became subdued. The surrender of Port Arthur was painful enough, but scarcely two weeks passed before news of a peaceful demonstration in St Petersburg ending with the massacre of hundreds caused a mixture of shock, resentment, suppressed excitement and bitterness.

'It's started,' Izzy whispered. 'They've got what they wanted – a bleedin' revolution! Just you see the way they're lookin' at you now. They know it's all goin' to change. They'll be watchin' you now real close!'

She could not help being aware of the way some of the men watched her intently as she passed down the lines of beds. She simply ascribed it to natural male curiosity and knew it was vain of her but could not deny a certain secret satisfaction at receiving such attention.

'It's not wot you're thinkin',' Izzy made clear. 'As I told you, it's wot name you 'ave.'

'What name?'

Something else was at work that he wasn't prepared to mention. In Nurse Daisy's opinion, the naturally suspicious Russians were now more certain than ever that the Mission was harbouring spies. This was so silly Alice laughed out loud. Izzy took it seriously. ''Course there are bleedin' spies!' he asserted. Defiantly she ignored it and went about her work more diligently and impassively than ever.

By ignoring it, she was also to a certain extent ignoring Izzy. He also appeared to ignore her for a while, finding all sorts of reasons to be away on 'business' on his own. It therefore came as a doubly hurtful shock when his discharge papers were delivered and he was grudgingly admitted to be 'Isaac King', loyal subject of His Britannic Majesty. Armed with his new identity and in a smart suit tailored especially for him, he travelled off to Mukden station within 24 hours of being notified. The cause of his absences, as it turned out, had been the making and fitting of a length of wooden leg and foot that he took pride in showing off to Alice just before leaving. He made her promise to visit him in Blackfriars. She gazed up into his earnest, smiling face and glistening brown eyes as he leaned down towards her from the cart and squeezed her hand.

With a wink and a nod he said, 'I done the best I can for you, Miss Alice,' passed her a packet and was gone.

It was assumed she had been in love with him. True, she had not been able to stop tears streaming down her cheeks when she waved goodbye. He had taken Leo's place in her affections even if the commitment had been no more than fleeting. She had loved his bright-eyed personality, his boyishness and his warmth. From time to time she had caught from the body heat imparted by his touch an inkling of the passion she knew could be awakened in her, which many of the wounded men offered her as well to a greater or lesser degree, and which played upon her as if she were an instrument ready to be taken from its case and strummed into intense, erotic, rapturous life.

Then one morning she bumped into Vassia as he came out of Uncle Elliott's bedroom, his solemn face alight with tears and his head shaking. Inside the room she glimpsed Dr Rawls folding something up. He saw her and signalled for her to come in just as the Chinese nurse was drawing a sheet over the bed.

7

Uncle Elliott was buried in the cemetery just below the rampart on the southern edge of the Mission's perimeter.

It was a windless morning of iron-hard frost. The distant river, iced over, shone like crystal in a luminous aura of cold sunlight without any sound of gunfire and perfectly suited to the thin hymn-singing chorus of voices rising in processional over the bare millet fields. They processed slowly behind the coffin and a large cross draped with lengths of white ribbon.

Bareheaded, the Reverend Gary Edstrom said prayers at the graveside, his tall figure in a black cassock oddly sinister against the crystalline brightness of the morning. After a short eulogy, followed by bible readings and a hymn, everyone watched the procedure of interment in a solemn silence broken only by a sudden burst of uncharacteristically loud wailing from the Chinese nurses who were all standing together shoulder to shoulder against the cold.

The quiet of the morning was similarly broken by a renewed distant booming of artillery as the ceremony ended and the procession reformed to return to the Mission.

Uncle Elliott's death left Alice with a bleak sense of her loneliness and her obligations. She knew she could now be free to go even if she mourned his death just as Elizabeth and Oliver mourned it, but hers was not the grief of a relative, nor of a colleague. Others had sensed it, she felt. Nikki Kozlov, saluting smartly, mentioned as much when the procession was over and everyone began to disperse at the Mission entrance.

'You will now be free, yes, Miss May?'

It was an odd thing to say and rather tasteless. In any case, why did he use her surname? She recoiled from the question's likely answer because at the same moment she noticed Oliver standing beside him, pale and tearstained.

'I have no intention of leaving, thank you,' she said, though the uncertainty in her voice was due to seeing the boy looking so sad. 'Oliver dear, aren't you...'

'My respects, ma'am.'

Nikki Kozlov was abrupt. He saluted again, this time with a click of the heels, turned away and left the Mission entrance, taking Oliver by the arm. She caught her breath as she watched the two of them striding off towards the eastern gate.

Elizabeth had said her brother spent so much time away from the Mission. Now she knew why. He was deliberately violating the Mission's policy of neutrality. Associating with Nikki Kozlov might not be a serious breach of the rules, since he was so frequent a visitor, but it made Alice aware how little care she had taken to keep her promise to look after Oliver. '*Determined*' was the word Uncle Elliott had used about him. She shrugged helplessly, thinking that there would be very little she could do to stop him if he was really determined to be a soldier, but she would do her best to stop him if she had the chance, and having determined that she walked off in the direction of the ground-floor ward.

Nurse Daisy was shaking a thermometer vigorously. She was paler than usual after being out in the cold for so long. Seeing Alice, she tried to hide her eyes.

'I know, I know, just don't ask! It's not like me to be like this. I *am*, though! Can't help it!' There were tears in her eyes. 'I been thinkin' it'd be best if... Heck, I dunno, maybe we shouldn't go on...'

Alice had never before seen her so upset and tried to comfort her.

'Sure, sure, I know. The Reverend Elliott, good, good man that he was, he wouldn't have had none of it – none of it! An' he'd be right!' Nurse Daisy ran the sleeve of her uniform across her eyes. 'I suppose we'll just keep our noses to the grindstone till it's all over. Still, with him gone…'

She looked round her at the men either lying in the metal beds or sitting round the stove, some two dozen in all.

'You know we're not here to do this sort of nursin', are we? These men need medical treatment in army hospitals, that's why Dr Leo should be here, shouldn't he?'

Alice of course agreed.

Nurse Daisy pushed the glass thermometer into its metal case and shook her head so impatiently the frilly bonnet waved about as if in a gust of wind.

'It never was meant to be like this! So now I dunno, maybe there ain't much sense in the Mission any more. What do you think, American Alice?'

Despite her own fears, she tried to reassure her and the effect was instantaneous.

'Sure, sure! I sure mustn't let it get to me! Lucy,' Nurse Daisy cried to one of the Chinese girls, 'I'll help! Chop-chop, basin… water… sponge!' Each word required pointing. 'Clean 'em up! That's right!'

So the business of the ward continued to Alice's relief, but another anxiety had been present in her mind even before Uncle Elliott's death. She had been shocked to find that in the little packet Izzy had given her, along with an advert for the Blackfriars shop, various keepsakes and his London address, there was a small, badly printed sheet of paper in Russian calling for soldiers to give up 'the stupid colonial war in Manchuria' and turn their guns to better use in 'destroying the seat of Imperialism, Tsar Nicholas II and his gang of bandits in St Petersburg.' She had seen other sheets like it and been told they were Japanese propaganda. But this one had at the foot of it, in small print, the single name **MAU**.

Her surname! In Russian!

Nikki Kozlov must have known about it. Was that why he had been so abrupt?

Was he warning her to leave?

Had he told Oliver?

Worse, did it have something to do with Leo?

But why, if Leo had written it, did he endanger her by using her surname?

Who else, though, would know her surname and use it like that?

These questions kept on flashing through her mind ever since she opened the packet. She had hastily torn up the sheet of paper into the smallest bits imaginable and kept only the sliver of paper with her surname on it. She knew it could be incriminating to keep even that scrap, but it seemed to her a sort of talisman of hope. If Leo was the author, the logic of love told her it could mean he wanted to keep in touch. After all, no one could reasonably suppose *she* had done it.

On the other hand, calm herself though she might with this thought, the surname was there, *her* surname, and even if it stood for nothing more significant than the month of May it could equally mean that Leo didn't care, her feelings didn't matter to him, it was a betrayal; and if it betrayed her, it seemed also to betray the very men whose lives were now her daily concern. Their truculence, their mutterings about being stabbed in the back by the revolution in St Petersburg, their mixture of self-pity and drunken, assertive boastfulness once Port Arthur had fallen, and their emotional nakedness which made them ready to shed tears – not, strictly speaking, from their wounds, nor from pain, but unaccountably, in a stolid, bewildered silence, and apparently unappeasably, with no one offering reproof or relief, pierced even Nurse Daisy's carefully erected defences against emotional involvement and quite simply flooded through Alice's like a rip tide.

None of the men was prepared to admit openly that defeat was imminent. Just across the Hun River new defensive earthworks were being thrown up. To the south and east, so Alice was told, there were successive lines of trenches that the Japanese would never be able to breach. Treason was there, though, as she could see clearly enough, in the depths of the men's eyes, along with the bewilderment and insecurity. Clutching crosses, little prayer sheets, lockets containing portraits of mothers, sweethearts, sisters, brothers, they seemed in need of a mother's comfort that neither she nor the local nurses could ever give. When they kissed her, they would no longer do it roughly as before but like supplicants to a priest, kissing the back of her hand or the edge of her skirt. It was only when they were discharged, mostly of course to be taken off on handcarts to the army hospitals by the station, that she looked down at their faces and felt her heart was being torn into little fragments as each one was carried off. She could not stop them coming, no more than she could stop them going. Each one of them, as if washed from her in a torrent, bled her heart a little.

One morning she was by the Mission entrance when she noticed a couple of tall Russian officers dressed in grey ankle-length greatcoats. They had revolver belts drawn tightly round their waists. It was unusual for firearms to be worn as openly as that virtually within the grounds of the Mission, but she thought nothing of it. Uniforms of every kind had become so conspicuous recently along with the increased noise and frequency of artillery exchanges that no one paid much attention.

Although her bonnet was visible, her own nurse's uniform was hidden beneath her new leather coat and she was assisting a soldier wounded in the foot to hobble his way towards a cart parked outside. At that precise moment her arm was seized. She turned, bridling, instantly defensive, and was surprised to find it was a girl reaching out to her. It did not dawn on her immediately what it could mean and was about to say something when the girl, obviously Russian, dressed in a fur coat and hat, anticipated her, spoke to the soldier and seemed deliberately to take over from Alice in helping the man towards the cart. The girl's behaviour and the way she looked back and smiled made no sense until there came the distinct sound of her name spoken in English.

'Alice...'

The voice took her completely by surprise. Not that she had not imagined it, nor tried over and over again to remind herself of it after hearing so many Russian voices, but now it sounded so ordinary she could not associate it with anyone in particular. He was standing there, at the very entrance to the Mission, in a swirl of snow. He was not one of the officers but it seemed he was with them.

'Leo!'

The name burst from her. At the first instant she hesitated. She did not know whether to run to him. It would be as if she were signalling for good that she was leaving what she had been and would be running in an ecstasy of hope and joy across a kind of no-man's-land into another world. But she did.

She ran through the crowd shouting 'Leo! Leo!' in a way she could never have expected of herself and on his broad, beardless, pale face a smile spread that looked as unexpected as her spontaneous race towards him. He held out his arms and she plunged into them and was enfolded by them.

Suddenly, after no search, as if Uncle Elliott's death or Izzy's departure had made it all come true, she found herself in Leo's arms. She never imagined she would be engulfed by such a strong physical compulsion the moment they met. Though it was a clumsy mutual hugging of fur and leather, of body trying to press against body, there was no denying the quick surge of desire. She was filled with a fierce, wanton craving for his lips and did kiss him there and then, in the middle of the crowd, and felt tremors of sheer excitement run through her body as if the pressure of his lips lit her full of sunlight.

Then, equally suddenly, she was shaken by uncontrollable gusts of laughter. The whole meeting, the circumstance, everything seemed so improbable she could not help herself, she laughed so much he laughed with her, his body shaking against hers, and it seemed they would both bend double at the stupendous joke.

Still laughing, she turned away a moment. Facing her there, within a couple of feet of her, was Mr Wei. His mask-like Chinese features glowed with a near-ivory pallor. Quick as a knife stroke the sight stopped her laughter. She gaped back at him in shock, shamed to think she had committed the unforgivable sin of levity.

He was still dressed all in white as a mark of mourning for Uncle Elliott.

In the certainty that he would rebuke her, she let go of Leo and tried to explain.

Instead Mr Wei bowed courteously. Even though he looked so pale and cold, he said with a smile, his lips quivering:

'Dear lady, I see... I see you are happy. May there be a thousand blessings on your happiness. Go with my boy. He will take you somewhere. Please... please go. I beg you.'

She could not believe what he was saying. To make his point clearer, he thrust towards her a boy of twelve or so, dressed like him all in white, and issued a stream of instructions. The boy immediately grabbed Alice's hand and tried dragging her after him through the crowd.

'But Mr Wei,' she protested, 'I've got to...'

'Hurry, hurry...'

Mr Wei waved at her. She saw then that the two officers were elbowing their way towards her. Seizing hold of Leo's hand, she pulled him as the boy pulled her. In a kind of wild, childish romp they formed a little human chain that went snaking through the crowds.

People yielded to them, more in astonishment, it seemed, than out of courtesy, alarmed by the boy's shrill shooing noises and the gruff shouts of pursuers. For Alice the zestful, uninhibited pushing and shoving of the boy and Leo's gasps and laughter at her side made her laugh and, still laughing, to the gaping, rather disapproving looks of Chinese bystanders, she ran up the tree-lined slope of ascending roadway to the city gate and through it and into a crowded street.

She remembered a particularly ferocious dragon on the corner of a building. Then, after several twists and turns, they were going down a narrow alleyway, pushing and shoving their way round handcarts, and then through a market area, the boy ahead no longer pulling but signalling vigorously, until they crossed a paved courtyard where pigs were snorting in a sty. Farther on, beyond doors, and down a long brick-floored passage, they were ushered into an apparently windowless, darkened room. All Alice could see were two astonished Chinese women who rose to their feet the instant they entered and bowed.

The boy made a series of rapid, breathless announcements, answered by the women with elaborate little flutterings of their hands and more bowing. At this point a large Chinese, his features creased and ancient, in a garment of shining silk with his arms folded across his chest, emerged through a screen door and welcomed them but pointed to their boots and outer clothing. They were being asked to remove them and they did so slowly, out of breath from the running, receiving more bows and smiles when the nurse's uniform was revealed. Moreover, there was no escaping the brisk removal of boots done expertly by the two women, who replaced them with little heel-less slippers. Beyond the screen door was another passage, this time carpeted, down which they were directed until they reached a screen door in a partition and were shown into a room.

In fact, though it had a shuttered window in one wall, the room was filled with a multi-coloured glow from a brazier in one corner that shed light as well as heat. Above it was a small ornate hood leading to a chimney set in the ceiling. There were red and gold silk hangings on the walls and the floor was strewn with elaborate cushions. Even though street noises could be heard, the room itself was warm and apparently insulated from the outside world.

'Dragon Throne.' Leo muttered.

She knew it was the hotel. Breathless, gulping the air that was faintly scented with incense, they stood and looked at each other. Then he stepped forwards and put his arms round her again.

They held each other close for a long time without saying a word. He was even more out of breath than she was and could do no more than shake his head with its damp, matted hair in a slow to-and-fro movement of disbelief and amazement. She took off her bonnet, shook out her hair and joined him as he fell to his knees and held up both hands to her. She knelt beside him and then both sank among the cushions, breathing deeply.

'I know I should have sent letters. I should have told you.'

'Oh, no.'

She gasped and pressed a finger to his lips. Seeing him as close as that, his clean-shaven jaws as neat and firm as a boy's contrasting so awkwardly with the sombre, worn look of the worry lines about his eyes, she could not help herself and ran the tip of her finger lightly over his cheeks and lips and brows. He was the Leo she had known but somehow reconstituted as someone grown artificially younger and more accessible to her, dressed as he now was in an army tunic, like so many of the young soldiers, but with a small red cross embroidered on the tunic's left chest. For that reason she found the need to speak irrepressible and the words began to bubble up inside her. In a rush she said:

'I know, I know... Leo dear, please let me, let me just say' – a gulp of breath – 'I didn't know where you were... or what might've happened. I honestly didn't know.'

Her tone changed quickly. But you *are* alive. We *are* alive. We *are* here. It was true, not a dream. It was the first time she had been so close to him, the first time she had been so close to anyone, let alone a man, since her mother died or since – the remembrance came quickly and startlingly like a gunshot – she had been seduced by the brother of the two girls who had nicknamed her Turtle, John, in the bedroom. Then the shame of it. She had vowed: *Never, never, if she could help it!* Then the changing patterns of coloured lights on the wall offered a different magic.

'Who was that girl?' she asked. 'The Russian girl? ...And those officers, who were they? I mean why did we have to run like that?'

'Please,' he said quietly as if about to explain something, but she checked him.

'Oh, it doesn't matter. But you *are* alive. We *are* alive. We *are* here.'

She was talking such nonsense, she acknowledged to herself, because this exotic, strange, Chinese room in which they were lying, with its brilliantly glistening lights changing from red to mauve to orange to yellow to gold, in the strange city of Mukden, in the middle of a war, could never be real. It could never be familiar, it could never be where she might expect to find him. She studied his face with the utmost care in the hope of absorbing its appearance before the dream gradually evaporated and took it from her. The scrutiny drew her attention to the smoothness of his skin along the jaw line and neck. The thick, still damp hair lay in streaks across his forehead.

But the main feature apart from the eyes beneath their straight brows was the remarkable mouth. Half open, the lips had a youthful, shapely fullness. They mixed sensuality and intelligence. In their fresh pinkness, enhanced by the weirdly variable light from the brazier, they were the central point of masculinity in his strong Russian features. She went on after a pause, more calmly:

'You probably know, don't you, about the Reverend Elliott Wyburn? You know he died? He was a great man. Without him there'd have been no American Mission. Of course, I can understand now why so many of his helpers left, but we're so short-staffed and there are so many wounded coming to the Mission. You're needed there more than ever. Nurse Daisy – remember her? – she said you'd be back. Like a bad penny.'

He was shaking his head. It was an indeterminate sign, hardly really negative, she thought, because she supposed he knew perfectly well what she meant, his eyes fastened on her in a steady blue-and-emerald gaze that might have suggested he was listening too hard.

'Yes, I heard.' He pointed to his ears.

'What?'

His silence while she talked had been interpreted by her, in a vague way, as a sign that he simply wanted to listen. So when she saw his hand shake as he raised it to his ear, she was suddenly filled with a new and terrible anxiety for him.

'What?'

'I cannot hear well. Explosions.'

'You can't hear?' She wondered if he had heard anything she said.

'Oh, I hear you, my dear. Most words. Forgive me.' He smiled weakly and his gaze wavered. 'Not to worry, as Miss Maddocks used to say. It was explosions. Japanese shells – bang! Very close. My ears…' He blinked at her as she rose on one elbow to look down at him. 'I thought I was deaf. But no… no, I thought I was going to die.'

He avoided her eyes as he mentioned this, as if he were a little ashamed of confessing it. She caught from him the sense that she would be prising open a part of him he wanted to keep completely to himself, completely shut, if she were to ask him questions about it.

'No, no, it is not important.' He once more seemed to anticipate and deter her reaction. 'Field surgery. Surgical work, very close to wounds. I need to see, not to hear. It is all. But I must ask forgiveness.'

'For what?'

'I do not speak English for… Oh, for how long? Weeks, yes? So forgive me if I do not use all your English "the's" and "a's" – *the* this and *a* that, you know?'

It was enough that he smiled. The estrangement of absence, all the anxiety about her feeling for him, the momentary doubts seemed to slip away like the quieting of an echo. She could understand exactly why he had found it hard to hear what she had been saying, not only because she had been speaking too fast but also because he had not spoken English recently. What mattered was that she had trusted her love and now she knew she had been right.

'Leo dear, I understand, I really do. It doesn't matter about that at all.'

She was going to say 'I do love you,' but he raised a finger to her lips almost in imitation of what she had done and the surprise movement stopped her.

'Listen.'

She thought he meant he wanted to say something of his own, but in fact he was listening.

'What?'

'Listen.'

Who was the deaf one? she wondered immediately because she had not noticed that raised voices could be heard somewhere in the carpeted passage. At first she thought they came from the street but then she recognised the voices were speaking Russian and growing louder. To her the words were incoherent. Leo maintained the pressure of his finger on her lips, blinking rapidly as he listened. She heard the hiss of something burning in the brazier.

'They look for us,' he whispered.

'Who?'

'Officers. Sh-sh-sh!'

She was instantly rigid with fear. The nape of her neck felt icy and a freezing cold puckered the skin of her scalp. She remembered the two officers by the Mission gates. Presumably it was their voices already resounding beyond the partition and being countered by a boy's voice. The exchanges between the deep Russian voices and the sharp contralto of the boy's suggested comic opera at first until it was clear the boy knew what he was doing. He was not just being courageous, he was also being clever.

'Plivate,' he was saying. 'Plivate... plivate... plivate.'

The repetition of the English word in his shrill voice and his refusal to admit that he even spoke Chinese, let alone Russian, seemed to have the effect of confusing the whole issue of cultural difference. No doubt he would be giving little bows each time he spoke, Alice thought, and that would add to the confusion. She wondered where the two women were or the large Chinese man and was then relieved to hear the boy say in his metallic, colourless voice:

'No! No! Plivate! No go here! No!'

By now the reiteration must have begun to impress the intruders. The Russian voices suddenly withdrew. There was silence on the other side of the partition. Practically immediately a sharp altercation between Chinese voices out in the street caused a release of tension.

'Why were they looking for us?' Alice asked.

'For me because... because they believe I am dangerous. For you because... because they believe you spy for Japanese.'

'Oh, I've heard nonsense like that before and it *is* nonsense!'

'No, no, my dear, it is true. I am dangerous because I know... because I know many people.' He leaned very close to her, smiling. 'My dear, my name now is different. I am Nikitin, yes, but I have two names now. For political reasons my name now is...'

It was then she judged from the way his smile became self-conscious what he actually meant. Knowing from recent experience a little about the subterfuges so common in Russian life, she anticipated him by suddenly reaching into the pocket of her nurse's uniform. He watched her in bewilderment.

'What?'

'I knew. I guessed.' She extracted the tiny sliver of paper and held it out to him.

'Ah-h-h!'

She explained about Izzy leaving it for her and how she had torn up the rest of the leaflet. It was as if she had caught him out in a dishonourable activity and was not surprised by the shamefaced way he smiled up at her.

'Politics, my dear,' he said as if talking to himself. 'You are not Russian. For you politics is not living and dying. For us, for Russians, politics is always living and dying. So we must hide who we are, hide our real names, if we want to protect ourselves from police, from spies, from enemies...'

The words had a chilling and distancing meaning for her the instant he spoke them. They spelled out the possibility that he had used her name not out of love but simply as a disguise. For a moment she searched his face anxiously but he sat upright and calmly seized her by the shoulders.

'You know why I am here? Something your friend Izzy said.'

'Izzy?'

'He was in hospital in Harbin. His amputation had become infected.'

'Infected! How?'

He raised an eyebrow. 'You were fond of him?'

She blushed very slightly. 'He was a real friend, yes.' So Leo was jealous! It brought a pang of joy.

'Was it badly infected, the amputation?'

'No, no. It will get better.'

'Oh, yes, he showed me the contraption made for him, of course...'

'Yes, it was why. How much were you fond of him?'

'Just fond, that's all.'

She could have resented more queries and her expression probably showed it. He pursed his lips into a tight smile.

'But he talks, your Izzy,' he whispered, 'and he talks too much. He said there was someone with your – *our* – name in Mukden. I knew I couldn't wait. I decided to come here at once. So I asked my nurse Arina Nikolaevna to come with me, she is my helper, you know, trained... No Takeo-san now. So she was with me...'

He cleared his throat and then went on:

'But we have been so busy. Hospital trains, field hospitals, operations in front line, since New Year in hospital in Harbin and now I must go to our hospital here in Mukden. My fingers now,' he waggled them, 'are very skilful. So until your Izzy King said May, I did not believe anyone knew your name. Your name has protected me. Your name in leaflets against war, against killing, against maiming, against wounds... Oh, it was just month of May! But no, it was your name and my name! I am May. Yes, I am May. I used you name. I am sorry.'

'Leo dear, you don't have to be sorry! I mean, I want the war stopped as much as you do and I understand...'

'No, I am sorry.'

He looked at her solemnly. She recognised that he wanted her to listen carefully to what he was about to say and she respected him for wishing to share not merely a confidence but a confession of self that gave meaning to his whole life. He lifted his right hand from her shoulder.

'I am Russian. We are emotional people, we Russians. We love drama. So look, I show you, with this hand I am doctor, I am surgeon. I will be doctor and surgeon all my life. I will always use my right hand to be doctor and surgeon. But my other hand, it takes risks. It is political. It is duty of everyone now, of every honest Russian now, to be political. I believe it. Anyone who can help to stop this war must do what he can to stop it. I believe it. But revolution – it is different.'

He blinked his eyes and gazed at her for a few moments.

'No one can stop revolution. We Russians have wanted revolution. Revolution is about millions of people wanting change and no one sure what change it will be. Constitutional democracy, constitutional assembly, socialism perhaps, communism perhaps, anarchism, populism, republicanism, what? Who knows what? Revolution is uncertainty mixed with hope. I want certainty mixed with promise...'

'Certainty?'

'Certainty, yes. One thing is certain. Japanese must attack. They must defeat us before our Baltic Fleet arrives. That is certain. And also certain is you must be safe. Because I am certain about my love. And I want my certainty mixed with your promise to go to America, to be safe, to be away from this war. Promise me!'

'But what about *us*, Leo dear? I can't leave the Mission now!'

She was about to say she could not leave on account of the promise made to Uncle Elliott but that commitment was all too fragile. There was no denying that America was her destination as much as it was her birth right.

'No, no you cannot desert, I understand,' he agreed. 'As for me, you must not worry!'

The intentness of his gaze illumined by the constant, subtly changing light from the brazier scared her momentarily into a fear that this might be their last meeting or perhaps if not their last, then so short-lived and unreal there would be no opportunity for her to say all the things she wanted to say. And suddenly he said something so extraordinary she knew there was no need to say anything more.

'I know what is most precious to me. So long as you are safe, I will be safe! Because I have married you, you see. We are both May.'

It was so unexpected and uttered so seriously, she was left breathless.

'What I have written is treason, I know,' he admitted. 'They know me as Dr Nikitin, surgeon. But I must be your name, too. Everywhere I go I see wounded and broken men and I try to help. I am known. I have good reputation. As for those leaflets, they do not know I wrote them but they know your name. You must say you know nothing. You will be safe in your Mission so long as you are there. But I cannot desert – you know what I mean? I cannot give up what I do. In wartime I must continue to do what I can to save men's lives. Afterwards, well...'

She leaned forward and kissed him. He looked for several moments straight into her eyes. Then he began again with a shake of the head.

'What fool I am, as Miss Maddocks used to say. But forgive me – for using your name.'

'Of course I forgive you!'

'Listen, my dear, I have no time. Today I must visit our Russian hospital here. I came to Mukden, you see, to persuade you…' Pressing his lips together, he smiled. Then he said: 'To persuade you that I love you and care so much for your safety and want you to leave and go to America. A safe conduct can be got for you and for …'

'No,' she cried, flinging her arms round his neck, 'if you stay, I stay! I am not going to desert. It's what you said.'

She drew back the instant she felt the hard material of his tunic collar. It reminded her of the many times she had felt the same material when undressing the wounded.

'How you can wear this I don't know!'

He was smiling back at her. 'How can I wear what?'

'This uniform.'

'I wish to be… ordinary soldier. But why do I wear it? Why do you wear yours?'

'Mine?'

'Yes. Why?' Very deftly he undid her collar button.

She laughed. It was an overture. 'You want me to take it off?'

'It is our revolution,' he whispered, undoing another button. 'Mrs May.'

'Oh, yes!'

It sounded too arch, but already her uniform was beginning to slip off her shoulders. She burst into soft, delighted, embarrassed laughter, joining with him in the slightly awkward manipulation of clothing and allowing him finally to draw her uniform free of her bodice and her shift until she lay there naked among the cushions. He looked down at her.

'Beautiful,' he whispered, kneeling above her and blowing her a kiss. Then with an alacrity that amazed her, he slipped off his belt, drew his tunic and shirt and vest over his head and undid his trousers. '*Sans culottes!*' he cried quietly and joined her among the cushions.

To see him naked made her glad to participate in his revolution as much as to assuage the long suppressed yearning for her own. The affirmation came with the urgency of their bodies' warm pressure against each other. She felt that *this*, the joy of nakedness, was a true fulfilment of her anxious love for him over so many weeks, that he should enjoy what his hands hungered for as they held her and stroked her, just as she had hungered in body and soul for his touch. His loving, appreciative caressing of her shoulders, her breasts, her spine, her mount and sex was a joy awaited with a sort of remote delight and now made real in an onrush of passion.

She felt plunged into warm soft seas. His body, firm and muscular against hers as he lifted himself, cleaved and overwhelmed her. She gave a gasp of surprise and joy when his sex filled hers and sent quick, flickering currents of pleasure through her. Her excitement mounted and mounted, matching his quickness and drawing him on, their gasps fighting each other from one stage of pleasure to the next, the cushions surrounding them joining in a soft applause of skin on silk that seemed to be repeated in the wavelets of colour elongating and merging and running together on the ceiling above her. She could not help herself. She dissolved into ecstasy and her body quivered as he lifted himself briskly from her.

Love no longer physical, not even truly emotional, but as if it were a whole new life engulfed her like a wave. In the wake of his withdrawal she knew she loved him more than she could ever have imagined. It had never seemed so strong or durable or complete as at that moment. She was delighted to be swamped by this wave of feeling.

For several moments they lay side by side exhausted, beached, it seemed, with the sea gone completely, until his speedy, medically efficient use of a handkerchief awoke her to the need to break the spell. They laughed in unison, like children caught in some flagrant naughtiness, as if the strong, animalistic scent and stickiness were so private it needed instant concealment, whereas to her it was like an anointing and she felt a kind of pride at receiving it. He rose above her and leaned down to her face and kissed her deeply. She flung her arms round his head and held him firmly to her as he kissed. She did not want to speak or break in any way the charmed ring of contentment surrounding them.

Then he sprang to his feet and began pulling on his clothes. It was what she knew should happen, but the curtailment of their loving seemed excessively needless and cruel. She quickly followed his example. Silently they both dressed, he quicker than her out of greater practice, she supposed. Within a short time, though she fumbled with her clothing, all thumbs suddenly, the dressing was done and they faced each other, smiling, as she did up the last buttons.

The screen door in the partition was drawn across almost inaudibly before anything could be said between them and the boy appeared. He bowed deeply. Even when he straightened himself, he stood only a little taller than their waists.

'Please to leave,' was his polite, solemnly uttered message. The women stood behind him holding coats and boots in readiness.

'I am going to stay,' she whispered quickly into Leo's ear. 'I came as far as this for my father's sake, I know. Now it is my choice. I choose to stay. I am staying for your sake.'

She could hear herself saying this in a voice that sounded firm and clear even though it was no louder than a whisper, but inwardly she was beginning to howl like a child. She drew back a little to study his face.

'I'm not going to leave you. Not after this. I'm not going to let you go.'

She caught her breath very sharply. The thought that the happiness of this unexpected meeting should end so abruptly, without any chance of renewal, seemed unendurable. Shaking his head, he lifted her towards him.

'We will meet,' he whispered. 'Remember we...'

They were being politely chivvied. The women had already held up their coats for them to put arms into sleeves. Then they began squatting down in front of each of them on their haunches. It would not be right, she knew, to prevail any more on their patience or the boy's discretion. As her fur-lined boots were being carefully replaced on her feet, Leo whispered:

'Remember, we are married. Secretly. But I have to do my work. And it will not be wartime forever.' He hugged her. 'Now I will go first. My dear, do not worry.'

'How can you expect me not to worry? I mean it's not...'

He adjusted his fur coat. 'Please,' he said.

She clenched her fists. She was determined not to shed tears in front of the Chinese. Yet the stricken look on her face seemed immovable. Though she could not fail to notice the strained, deliberately rigid expression that gripped his features and kept him dry-eyed as well, she softened. She unclenched her fists and tried to hold him, but he slipped from her and moved away, giving a little wave that in its fluent, easy wrist movement was somehow confident and debonair. Then he stuffed the fur hat on his head and went into the passage.

Silhouetted for a moment in the rectangle of the screen door, his black bulk against the white background light, he paused and she was on the verge of calling out his name, *their* name, but he went through the door and disappeared.

8

'Russia men!'

The Chinese girls bowed, speaking almost in unison.

'Russia men come!'

The girls averted their eyes when asked anything more. Usually so open and friendly, they resisted all Alice's enquiries as if ashamed to answer, but it was soon obvious why.

Opening the door to her bedroom, she saw it was in a mess. Her bible, for instance, had been flung into a corner under the washstand, the framed photograph of her great-grandmother had been smashed, her suitcase turned upside down and clothes strewn about, all done, it seemed, very hurriedly, judging by what she saw at first glance. Obviously it had been searched by those referred to as the 'Russia men' whom the girls were too ashamed to admit they had let in, though Alice was instantly certain they were the officers who had been following Leo.

Why they had been allowed to enter the Mission so freely, let alone make such a mess, was shocking, but Alice knew that if she complained it could mean she was under suspicion. Her name, her relationship with Leo, not to mention her love for him, the likelihood she might never see him again, all combined to be mirrored in the tumble and whirl of the flakes she stared at through the window. They reflected the doubts and choices facing her, paltry though the tiny white snowflakes were by comparison with the excited, constantly changing lights she had glimpsed only so recently, flickering and blending on the ceiling of the room in the Dragon Throne hotel, but they were better to watch than the mess surrounding her.

The bedroom, after all, was now hers. Elizabeth had moved all her belongings into what had been Uncle Elliott's room. The change had apparently been the dying man's wish since uncle and niece had grown very close in his last days. All his photographs and clothes and mementoes had been carefully packed away in trunks to await the time they could be shipped to California.

Alice banged the door shut behind her and barricaded herself in. With a wooden chair jammed against the door handle, she started mechanically doing what she knew best, which was to tidy the room as quickly as possible to distract herself from thinking too much about the wretchedness of it all. The small bedside table was put back in its place along with her parents' silver-framed photograph and her great-grandmother's, now without its glass. All her few dressing-table items, swept onto the floor during the search, were put back. She tidied her clothes. Then she washed, dressed, wiped away tears and, refreshed, leaned her forehead against the cold windowpane in an effort to recover calmer feelings.

She felt more trapped than ever, if that were possible. The Mission was both her home and her prison. It offered a lifeline to Leo while simultaneously confining her hopes within the limited daily round of nursing duties and yet also, by contact with the Russian wounded, laying her open to suspicion, loss of privacy and exposure to the indignity of such searches. Izzy would have known what to do!

A tap on the door startled her. In sudden fright she asked who it was.

'Oliver.'

The chair was moved. She drew open the door cautiously and peered through the slit. There he was in the hallway, dressed in the same large fur coat he had been wearing at the Mission entrance after Uncle Elliott's funeral. The straight line of the fur hat across his forehead emphasized his square features and the glowing blueness of his eyes. Of course, they had seen each other at mealtimes and often enough at other times, but she had hardly ever seen him in the house.

'Oliver,' she asked 'what?'

In the fading afternoon light of the hallway he looked suddenly very mature. A tautening of the skin over his cheekbones as well as his raised chin emphasised a boyish militancy in his features. He seemed older, even adult. She had always been fond of him and it pleased her to feel that the fondness was renewed between them in the instantaneous meeting of their eyes.

'You know what happened?'

'What?'

'Officers, Russian officers. They had a w-w-warrant...' Certain words still caused him to stammer. He gave an embarrassed flick of his head as if he were shaking the word free of his lips. 'They were shooed out of the hospital ward and came here. To search your room. You weren't here. So...'

'Yes, I had gone into Mukden.' She said it quickly, perhaps in too great a haste so as not to mention Leo. 'I can't understand why they were allowed into the Mission.'

'They've g-got a r-right to go anywhere, you know. If they think there are Japanese spies.'

She was scornful. 'So they thought there were Japanese spies in my bedroom!'

'It *is* your bedroom now, isn't it?'

'Yes.'

She was fearful he might know the likely reason, but he anticipated her.

'I sent them away. I said you were an American and it's an American Mission. I said we're all American here. Kozzer said it's what I must say. They won't be any trouble after this.'

'Kozzer? Oh, yes, your nickname for Captain Kozlov!'

'Nikki, Kozzer, yes...'

'Well, thank you, Oliver dear! So you sent them away!'

'Yes. And you're all right, are you?'

She told him she had never felt better and in an impulse of gratitude kissed him on both cheeks. He blushed and broke into a smile.

'M-m-must be going,' he stammered, waved and went out through the front door.

Her lips still felt the unexpected softness of the down on his cheeks. It reminded her at once of the feel of Leo's skin, that there was in that modest hirsuteness a sense of mystery and allure, of a man's love, for which she yearned again as a guarantee of all she had just experienced.

She pulled on her overcoat. When she returned to the hospital, Mr Wei had explained her absence by saying she had been on a mission of mercy in Mukden.

'Oh, yeah,' said Nurse Daisy, giving her a look. 'And did the patient recover? What's your secret, American Alice, eh?'

A gust of laughter followed. No mention was made of the Russian officers. For her part, she closed her mind to certain things. Nagging though it was, the curiosity to know about Leo's relationship with the young nurse Arina or all his other relationships seemed far less important than the comfort of knowing he loved her. What she could not put aside was the promise she had made to Uncle Elliott to look after his nephew. Every time she saw the empty bed in her bedroom she was reminded of his quiet voice speaking to her in the room now occupied by Elizabeth.

A couple of days later she bumped into Oliver in the hallway. He usually came and went at times when she was on ward duty and this encounter was accidental. He had just come in from outside. She thanked him once again. Blinking rapidly at her mention of the Russian officers, he brushed snow off his fur coat and glanced quickly round in embarrassment.

'I can't tell you about it here.'

This was said in a whisper. She noted how his eyes, as blue as a summer sky, shone into her face as if seeking out her trust and seemed to be satisfied by what they saw. He pointed to the hatchway in the ceiling.

'I'll tell you.'

She knew it was his home and he demonstrated as much by springing up in the air to release the catch holding the hatchway cover. It swung down along with a length of rope, followed in an instant by the almost soundless descent of the ladder. Like a large furry creature, his coat still damp from the snow, he dashed up into his hole and lowered a hand to help Alice up behind him. It was a sign of trust. No one else, so far as she knew, had ever been invited into his lair.

'Welcome,' he said a little uncertainly as he pulled her up. 'Please.'

The attic space was a quite large area of bare floorboards between a stove chimney at one end and a large boxed-in water tank at the other, the whole lit by a roof window. Apart from its coldness, what confronted her first was the slept-in fug of a boy's room. Then she saw an ancient wicker chair, a washstand with white jug and bowl, a bucket, a camp bed and a curtained alcove. Most of the sloping ceiling space was covered by a display of maps of the war in

Manchuria and magazine illustrations of recent battles stuck to the wooden cladding with strips of gummed paper. She also caught sight of a carefully coloured representation of the twin-headed imperial eagle, below which was hanging an officer cadet's peaked cap and what looked like a bayonet.

'I can close it all up if I want to.'

He demonstrated what he meant by quickly drawing up the ladder through the hatchway on a pulley and showing her how, with the ladder raised, he could close the hatchway cover and seal himself off from below.

'That's why I like it up here. I can be private, you know.'

He offered her the wicker chair, which turned out to be creaky and rather uncomfortable, while he squatted down on the low camp bed. From his manner as well as the fair-haired stubble down on his chin and cheeks she recognised he was no longer the slightly awkward, shy boy who had been her companion on the train journey. He stammered a lot less frequently and had acquired certain graces. Maybe it was because, she thought, he was no longer under his sister's thumb.

Sharing a bedroom with Elizabeth until so recently, she had heard little save complaints about Oliver's habit of flouting the Mission rules by visiting Mukden as and when he wished. The ostensible reason may have been to help Mr Wei, but his association with Nikki Kozlov had become common knowledge.

'Tell me about these officers, what the girls called the "Russia men".' she asked immediately. 'Do you know who they are?'

He looked at her from under his brows.

'No.'

She couldn't be sure whether he was telling her the truth. 'You said Captain Kozlov – you call him Kozzer...'

He said he was no good at pronouncing Russian names. Anyhow, the Captain didn't mind being called Kozzer. He grinned broadly.

'No, all right. I just wondered how well you know him and what he'd told you about the officers.'

'They're police people, I think. Anyhow, Kozzer doesn't like them.' He pursed his lips before adding: 'If they didn't steal anything, then it's best nobody says anything, don't you think?'

'Oh, yes, I entirely agree. It was good of you.'

The remark drew a temporary line under the episode. An extended silence ensued between them that was gradually filled for Alice with so many doubts her teeth began to chatter slightly as much from anxiety as from cold. On the point of saying something, she heard the chapel clock suddenly strike four. It had never sounded so loud, since her bedroom was on the other side of the house, and she put her hands over her ears.

'You have to sleep through that, do you?'

'I'm used to it.' He smiled and ran his tongue round his lips. 'It's worth it so I can be myself.' It was said matter-of-factly and in an archly defiant way. 'Because of this.'

'What?'

The maps and pictures were indicated. Because they infringed the Mission's policy of neutrality, they had been torn out of magazines and newspapers delivered to the library. She lowered her voice, knowing the lengths to which the policy had been taken:

'Let me guess – you've done all this without Gary Edstrom knowing…'

'I don't care what that Gary person thinks!'

In a flash he was truculent and angry in a way she had never expected.

'Oliver dear!'

He turned his face to her in profile, evidently going red. What he then said was a teenage litany of complaints about being asked questions and told what he must do, how his sister had harped on and on about his flouting the rules, how Gary Edstrom had told him to stop seeing Kozzer. Alice had never guessed so much pent-up anger had been generated. She tried to hazard a reason.

'You know your sister loves him, don't you? Is that what's annoying you?'

'I *know* Liz is soppy about him, but I'm not. He thinks he has a right to b-b-boss me. He says I can't leave the Mission. He says we've all got to be neutral. He says the war is just a war between two emperors, between two so-called empires…'

His angry confessional mood led him to chop the air with his right hand at each statement. Alice tried to soothe him.

'Oliver dear, there's still time.'

'Time for what?'

'Time for you to leave. Time for us to leave. I mean, we could still go to California…'

She knew she was beginning to sound insincere, if only because she had no intention of taking such a step herself. He pulled a face.

'Would you?'

Confronted like that, she had to grin self-consciously and shake her head.

'So I'm not going! No, I'm not going to quit!'

'Quit the Mission, you mean?'

He tore off his fur hat. 'Quit what we have to do.'

'What's that?'

He ran his fingers through his fair hair, ruffling it into what, to her, was its more usual fullness after it had been so compressed by the hat and gazed up at her with a grin. He had leant forward with an elbow on one knee and his chin resting on the back of his hand, determined, it seemed, to convince her and spoke so airily, so self-confidently, she could hardly believe she was listening to the stammering boy she had learned to trust as a friend.

'There's something I've got to do and something you don't know. I bet you can't tell the difference?'

'What difference?'

'Between Chinese and Japanese.'

'But there *aren't* any Japanese here!'

She was so sure of this that his immediate response of saying nothing bewildered her by highlighting both his scepticism and the likelihood that she might be wrong. His clear blue eyes gazed at her a little sadly.

'Yes, there are.'

'How do you know?'

'I do, that's all. You're too nice, Alice, you can't *see* what's happening. There's going to be a big battle and we've got to be prepared. Well, I'm prepared, anyhow.'

'Prepared?'

'Yes. And I know what I've got to do.'

'Prepared – what do you mean?'

He placed his hands together in a preacherly manner.

'God is on our side,' he intoned. 'God is going to defend us. Jesus Christ is on our side.'

'What *do* you mean?'

'The Russians are Christians. They are fighting for Christianity. So I have decided...' He stuck out his chin. 'I have decided to be a Christian s-s-soldier! Now promise you won't tell anyone!'

'But Oliver...'

'Promise you won't tell Liz! Or that Gary person!'

She gave her promise, too troubled by his intentness to do otherwise. He jumped to his feet.

'Look!'

Proudly he whisked back the little curtain in the alcove formed by the angle of the roof to reveal an army tunic, belt, trousers and greatcoat.

'This is my armour... my armour of righteousness!'

Alice could do no more than stare at the array with the blank amazement of someone suddenly confronted by signs of unspeakable tastelessness in a loved one. As an armour, it looked tawdry, the same coarse material she had come across so often on the wounded and seen on Leo. That he should describe it so grandiosely and in such a crusading spirit merely emphasised his immaturity.

'Look!'

He held the tunic up against his chest, evidently seeking her approval.

It was clearly too large, but this did not concern him as much as Alice's silence.

'What do you think?'

'I think it's too large.'

She said it quite honestly and he gave her an awkward smile. Then he returned the tunic to the alcove, drew back the curtain and once more squatted on the camp bed.

'You're not going to tell anyone, are you?'

She shook her head, trying to muster her thoughts. She knew he had done her a great favour but she could not bring herself to say anything.

'You know I want to be a s-s-soldier. This is the only chance I'll have to be in a real war. So I'm going to join the Russian army. It's all arranged now.'

'Oh, but you can't! Oliver, you can't!' The cries were spontaneous as protest welled up inside her. 'You absolutely mustn't!'

'Why can't I?'

'You're not old enough!' She remembered Uncle Elliott's plea to her.

'Yes, I am! Kozzer says there are boys of my age in the Russian army.'

'I see.'

'We play chess. He has a room in the Dragon Throne hotel… I've been there a lot. I've always had my own friends. I'm going to do what *I* want. I'm going to join the Russian army.'

She recognised he was challenging such guardianship as she might still have over him in saying this, but more seriously he was defying the goodwill of the Mission. At a loss for anything to say, she looked round her and was surprised by glimpsing a lead soldier he had brought with him from London. The toy marched stiffly in red and black uniform along a short shelf fixed to the back of the washstand, next to a tooth mug with a toothbrush handle protruding from it. The sight made her swallow.

'You mustn't! You absolutely mustn't! Oliver dear, you're only a boy!' The spontaneous scolding tone of her voice caused her to stop. Then she added more calmly: 'We *are* fond of you, you know. I'm very, very fond of you, Oliver dear, and so is Elizabeth. And what would your uncle have said…'

'Oh, Liz couldn't care!'

'No, that's not fair. You're not being fair to any of us, least of all to your sister. I know she complains about you. But I don't want to see you hurt. Do you know what some of the wounds are like? Have you seen any of them?' He shook his head. The afternoon light had faded so much they were both sitting in semi-darkness. 'And you won't have any special protection if you join the army.'

'Kozzer says he'll be like a father to me. He'll look after me,'

She was touched by his faith. She pointed out that they would also look after him in the Mission. He gave a short and surprisingly cynical laugh.

'I know you will, but Liz, she's too fond of... Oh, it d-d-doesn't matter! I know perhaps d-d-deep down she cares, but we have different feelings now, we're not thinking the same way any more...'

His gaze appealed to her for understanding. She knew exactly what he meant, no matter whether it could be summarised as resentment of his sister's infatuation or an awareness in himself of a chemistry that made the incompatibility so obvious; or perhaps, more than this, his own craving for reassurance and guidance, not to mention what he rather doubtfully claimed as his armour of righteousness, and she spontaneously reached out and seized his hand:

'Please, for my sake, Oliver dear, for your uncle's sake, don't do anything like that! Please don't! Your Uncle Elliott made me promise to look after you. He was worried, very worried about your determination to be a soldier. *Determination*, that's the word he used. He wished you wouldn't, you know.'

He let his hand be squeezed for a moment and then withdrew it deliberately.

'I promised Kozzer.'

'Oh, really, Oliver dear...'

'I promised. I'm not saying anything more.'

He was duly respectful of her pleading but she easily detected in his words and his gesture a natural stubbornness and masculine scorn of her qualms.

In the silence they heard the noise of the guns.

*

She listened out for the hatchway being opened during the next few days and heard it more than once, but since she did not see him she assumed the true extent of his apostasy was not known. For a while the matter did not cross her mind. She was too preoccupied with work on the ward and perhaps too selfishly concerned (as she privately admitted to herself later) with her own feelings. Suddenly one morning, as she was helping Nurse Daisy, she received a summons to go to the 'office', meaning the administrative centre of the Mission.

Alice never found out how Oliver's treasures had been discovered. They were there in a box on the desk, the bayonet lying on top of the pictures and maps and the folded Russian uniform. On one side of the desk sat Gary Edstrom and Elizabeth, on the other side stood Oliver very upright, defiant, his jaw raised and his expression stern and unblinking. The total effect clearly overplayed his longed-for show of martyrdom.

'Alice, I want to keep this in the family.' Gary Edstrom did not trouble to welcome her. His tone was business-like, but fractious. 'I think you know what I mean. We mustn't let it get about that, well… Look, these things! They just cannot be allowed, you know!'

He picked up the bayonet in gloved fingers, dropped it back into the box and asked her if she had ever seen it or any of the other military items.

She made an effort to peer at them conscientiously. It seemed right to her to protest at being summoned to this inquisition, but the 'office' was so cold and the atmosphere so fraught she found herself furiously debating which would be the better course for Oliver's sake – to admit the truth or deny everything. Obviously something had happened – a showdown of sorts between them, she supposed - and the two sides were now suddenly drawn up in the battle lines of this unequal face-to-face confrontation. She rummaged around in the box and then remarked that the pictures and maps all seemed to have been torn out of newspapers and magazines.

'Yes, yes!' This was dismissed as trivial. 'I mean the Russian uniform, the army cap, the bayonet…'

His attitude of over-zealous distaste for such things so upset her she composed her features into a candid show of innocent honesty.

'They're probably just items left by some of the wounded…'

'So you're not sure you've seen any of these things before?'

'I can't be sure I've ever seen *these* things. I've seen lots like them.'

'Alice, please,' Elizabeth said. 'Didn't you see them up in Ollie's room? He said he showed them to you.'

She could not meet Elizabeth's gaze. A consuming sense that everything had suddenly become back-to-front, that here she was being forced into telling lies for Oliver's sake when she knew the truth only too well and wanted to dissuade him as much as anyone, filled her heart to the brim and brought tears to her eyes.

The 'office' itself, in its chill, chapel-like silence, in the very fact that they were all wearing outdoor clothes, felt as bleak as the picture of snow-covered shrubbery visible through the window and was repeated by an equivalent interior bleakness of shelves full of book spines and folders and ledgers, a small stars-and-stripes flag pinned to the wall, a silver cross beside it, impersonal framed photographs of formal staff groups, a very stilted posed photograph of Uncle Elliott. It all provoked in Alice a reluctant conviction that they were becoming frozen in their attitudes.

'He showed me a uniform, yes.'

Gary, infuriated, wagged a finger at Oliver. 'But you admit it's yours, don't you?'

Shakily but proudly Oliver answered: 'I am going to be a Christian s-s-s-soldier!'

The forced sibilance of his effort to pronounce the word had an unintentionally comic effect. Elizabeth broke into a trill of laughter.

'Which means what?'

Over the sound of Gary's angry voice and Elizabeth's self-conscious giggles Oliver spoke out loudly:

'I am going to be a Christian s-soldier! I intend to fight for a Christian cause. Aren't we all Christians? Aren't the Russians Christians? Don't they f-f-f-f-..' A rapid flick of the head as if avoiding an insect '.. f-fight for their religion? Liz, shut up!'

'Oh, all right, all right, I'm sorry.' She began wiping tears from her eyes.

'Oliver, we are all Christians. But we are peace-loving Christians,' said Gary Edstrom.

'Christians must defend their faith.'

'I know that, Oliver, I know that. But we must be neutral here in the Mission…'

'Oh, you're being so silly, Ollie!' Elizabeth broke in, mastering her laughter. She waved a handkerchief up and down in front of her as if she literally waving goodbye. 'I know you've always wanted to be a soldier. But we're both just guests of the Mission and we've got to do what we're told. Gary knows about these things, you don't. You're not old enough! You're not yet sixteen! You're hardly more than a little boy! So do stop being so silly! Take all this stuff away! Get rid of it!'

To Alice the moment was decisive. She knew then it had all been Elizabeth's doing, no doubt for the best of reasons. Oliver suddenly forestalled her own desire to protest by looking expressionlessly at his sister for several seconds and then stepping forward without a word, gathering up his box of things and stalking towards the door.

Elizabeth jerked herself to her feet, calling out:

'Ollie, please!' Her pretty face wore an expression of remorse and shame.

'Elizabeth, you shouldn't have! Not to your brother! He doesn't deserve it!'

These exclamations startled Alice as she uttered them. She inhaled deeply and exchanged a momentary glance of sheer anger with the girl. Elizabeth sat down abruptly without a word. Alice went on in a voice quivering with anger. She addressed Gary Edstrom, aware that Oliver was still in the room:

'You wanted to keep it in the family. I know he is very stubborn and determined, but he mustn't be treated as a little boy. He has ideas of his own. He showed me his things and I promised not to tell anyone and I haven't. Oh, yes, I know he shouldn't be a soldier! What he needs is love! His mother died when he was – what? Eight? He's needed a mother's love and nannies and tutors haven't been enough. That's why he stammers. No, he doesn't deserve to be scolded! We all need love at a time like this, we need mercy, we need to care, don't we?'

Elizabeth suddenly burst into tears. 'Oh, I know you're right! I'm sorry, Ollie, I really am!' She began sobbing.

Gary Edstrom patted her on the shoulder in a somewhat awkward and perfunctory gesture that signalled clearly enough how little comfort he could give and simultaneously rose slowly to his feet, leaning forward with both gloved hands palm-downwards on the desk. His voice was calm, amiable and tinged with tiredness in evident performance of a painful duty.

'Alice, my dear, we cannot have bayonets and army uniforms in the Mission, you know that as well as I do! We cannot allow it! Oliver, get rid of the stuff, please! And for the love of God – I mean it – put aside your ambition to be a soldier! For our sake, for your sister's sake, for everyone's sake!'

Alice swung round to look at Oliver still holding his box. She knew nothing said by Gary Edstrom would placate him and he simply stared back straight-faced before giving a loud sigh and walking noisily out of the room in hobnailed boots. She caught up with him on the frozen pathway outside, bruised by the whole experience and in no mood to pander to him. He glanced over his shoulder, showing her a pale, angry face.

'Oliver dear, please! You know you shouldn't! Get rid of those things!'

He walked off some way, as if ignoring her, then looked back and called: 'Traitor!'

'Oliver, listen, I honestly didn't say a word!'

'You're all traitors!' he cried indignantly. 'You're all betraying Christ by not being prepared!'

He has gone mad, she thought, but she could muster no words beyond referring to his uncle. 'Your Uncle Elliott – surely you wouldn't want to offend him? He'd never let you do this!'

'My Uncle Elliott would understand. He wasn't namby-pamby like that Gary person. This Mission isn't worth anything if it isn't Christian.' He shifted the box in his arms. 'Someone has to be a Christian soldier!'

This was announced triumphantly. He heaved the box on to one shoulder and carried it ostentatiously off across the yard, giving a wave with his free hand.

'Oliver!'

He paid no attention. Chinese nearby looked inquisitively at both of them. She watched his slim figure in the outsize fur coat, with one arm raised carrying his armour of righteousness on his shoulder, move away from her with a ballet dancer's grace and go out through the Mission entrance. She knew exactly where he was going.

*

The little episode brought no truce. Formally polite relations with Gary Edstrom rather than warmth seemed hardly to matter in the light of what was happening on the ward, daily becoming more crowded. Elizabeth herself sought consolation from Alice by apologising for what she had said. The facts remained unalterable: Oliver had left the Mission; he did not come back; he would not be met in the hallway again, nor would his hatchway open and the ladder descend. Blame could be allotted at will. Alice blamed herself, Elizabeth blamed herself. The only alternative was to accept Mr Wei's information and Captain Kozlov's oddly accented assurances that the boy was being looked after.

For Alice there was a reminder in what her mother had often said: '*Cut the cackle! Cut curiosity in half!*' So she did not ask questions about Oliver, just as she did not torture herself about Leo. In London the embarrassment of not really understanding the little protocols of society life had been like walking naked and blindfold over a thick carpet of primness and politeness. Eventually she had worn the clothing of her mother's ill health as an excuse for not taking part.

The daily routines of the ward now had a surface simplicity. What had been Christina Arbuckle's little domain of the storeroom adjacent to the ward and the kitchen became the place where Nurse Daisy Royal and Dr Francis Rawls chatted and relaxed and ate and Alice was initiated into the coded, almost telepathic mode of communication between them, evolved over long acquaintance. It was as complex and secretive as the very contents of the storeroom. Accessibility would have been hard for a stranger, except that the code was American, ebullient, quick, unsophisticated, funny, unstuffy and, to Alice, easily understood and appreciated. She was joyfully grateful to be accepted as a friend and allowed to penetrate the wall of privacy they had erected round their lives.

It was based on good-natured banter without any emotional undertone. They told Alice they had first met through the joshing of colleagues about the similarity of their names – Rawls and Royal. The resulting playfulness had kept their relationship fresh and lively. Alice enjoyed their medical talk, their private allusions to little jokes and encounters in their mutual past, their reminiscing about the places they had been and their constant interest in their present surroundings. Once outside the Mission they simply regarded themselves as tourists. Alice accompanied them on expeditions like those she had made with Izzy and soon realized that their exaggerated bonhomie and noisy good fellowship should never be taken at its face value. It was an artful cover for a very solid professional competence and a magnanimous readiness to deal even-handedly with all and sundry, regardless of nationality, background or culture.

Casually one day Alice mentioned spies. Nurse Daisy roared with laughter.

'Gal, you've gotten just like them Russkies, bless 'em!'

'Why?' It bothered Alice to hear her say such a thing.

'They sure are spooked!'

'Spooked?'

'Spooked. So they're seein' things, know what I mean? We got spooked last fall. Practically every man, woman and child left here. We was spooked by the Japs. Thought they'd be here rightaway after Sha Ho. But they ain't started their attack yet. I respect 'em, you know. The way they fight!'

'But there aren't any here, surely. Not here, I mean, in the Mission?'

Nurse Daisy rocked her head from side to side. 'I sure wouldn't swear to tell one from t'other if they didn't have no numbers on 'em!'

She referred to the way the Chinese orderlies wore numbers on their coats. With masks over their faces it was hard to tell one from another.

'Which of 'em's a Chink and which a Jap?' she hissed in Alice's ear. 'Darned if I know.'

The question acquired a different meaning a few days later when a party of three Japanese prisoners arrived. One of them had suffered severe burns and needed very careful nursing care. The other two were stretcher-bearers. They stood there in the reception area surrounded by half-a-dozen Russian guards with fixed bayonets. The rule about surrendering weapons at the entrance seemed to have been relaxed in this case.

The Japanese looked neat, compact and small beside their captors. One stretcher-bearer was clearly more frightened than the other and his darting brown eyes went to and fro like marbles in a slot. The other smiled almost as vigorously, gave little bows and muttered a few French phrases. It turned out he had been a waiter in a leading Tokyo hotel before joining the army. Alice studied them closely, as did everyone else, and realized she could very easily have mistaken them for Chinese in uniform had she not known any better.

The injured man had serious burns. Alice followed Dr Rawls into the operating theatre, recently so little used, where he tut-tutted and sighed as he put on his mask and bent down to study the man's injuries through gold-rimmed spectacles. Delicately using tweezers, he set about carefully removing pieces of charred clothing that had been burned into the skin. The dreadful process was somehow worsened by the stoic silence of the victim. Apart from contorting his mouth and squeezing his eyes tight shut, he endured in silence as Dr Rawls, perspiring hard despite the cold, peeled back strip after strip of raw skin.

Suddenly, to Alice's surprise, he gave up. He nodded briefly to one of the medical orderlies and, turning away, tore the mask from his face. The man took over immediately with the evident confidence of a professional and bent his bespectacled face very close to the wounds to remove pieces of skin dexterously and competently, working the tweezers with a light plucking movement. As he did this he spoke soft words, apparently talking to himself, but the injured man's eyes watched him in gathering hope, his whole expression seeming to relax. It was a procedure that Alice could only follow with growing admiration at such a display of skill and care.

The moment two of the Chinese nurses began to apply dressings everyone's attention was diverted towards the adjoining ward. The Japanese stretcher-bearers had been given buckets of water for washing. It was a common practice. All new arrivals, if they were capable of doing so, were required to wash, since their uniforms were usually filthy and in need of delousing. This time the Japanese astonished everyone by carrying the request to its logical extreme.

They stripped naked and began soaping themselves all over. Oblivious of the peering Russian eyes, they offered a sight of healthy, uninhibited nakedness. Even the one whose eyes had darted in such fear only a short while before now confidently devoted himself to covering his stocky bronze frame with white soap suds.

The initial reaction was a few titters and guffaws, but soon the unashamed, candid enjoyment of the Japanese caused a spontaneous change of mood. One man with a bandaged head rose up slowly, cast aside his nightshirt and called out for more water. Men peered out from beds and two-tiered wooden bunks and the less seriously injured began stripping off. Soon there was a fraternising of naked bodies, a bacchanalia of pinkly white and tawny bronze skins, of gleaming buttocks and backs, of lurid scars, wildly flying strips of bandage and water spilling across the brick floor. In it all, in the laughter, in the friendly slapping of hands against bare skin there was no more than the boisterous horseplay of a bath-house.

The Chinese girls went into fits of giggles. Nurse Daisy contemplated the scene with a broad smile so long as it remained a cleansing process involving a good deal of slapping of wet clothing against naked skin for want of birch twigs and a certain amount of cavorting close to the stove. The small Japanese were soon swept to one side as an uproarious party-like atmosphere spread among the men regardless of their injuries. In an instant vodka bottles were being upturned into mouths, everlasting friendship was being proclaimed, energetic talk about freedom broke out and, smiling and laughing, the men sat around half-dressed on their beds seeming to have acquired by their very cleanliness a new identity and pride.

For the general entertainment one sprightly chap even attempted a dance. His efforts were quickly surpassed by a broad-chested young man, his arm in a sling, who climbed to his feet and launched slowly into the opening bars of a song. Alice had never heard it before. The singing voice breached the ripples of laughter and conviviality, overwhelmed the surrounding noise and gave rise to a deeply surging stream of sound, as spontaneous as it was rich. Gradually men's voices rose in the wake of the deep bass and caught up the words until they formed a choral tide. The movement quickly became a slow-flowing river of sound that spread out in majestically swelling, rolling, succeeding billows of resonant male voices audible throughout both wards, the reception area and the Mission yard.

At first strong and upbeat, it gradually became thinner and sadder as the trail of voices following the bass voice drunkenly elongated the plangent cadences of the song. Father Ambrosius, the priest who now visited the Mission regularly, crossed himself before the icon in one corner of the ward and showed a face covered in tears. All the Chinese staff pressed together in the doorway and the adjoining passage seemed totally absorbed in their listening.

It was as if the voices sang not only of heartache and sadness, not only of regret at the waste of life, but also of an exultant and uplifting change. Alice saw a transfiguration on the men's faces, as if there shone through them, like the pulsing of the music, an ever-growing radiance. The ragged choruses spoke at first of solitary figures climbing on a rock face, mounting slowly upwards out of darkness into light. They followed the throbbing, rising voice of the young bass singer as it ascended towards a triumphant climax, a peak of sound suggestive of dawn light gleaming from the topmost rock itself, and then, in its wake, the chorus of voices deepened into a murmurous yearning that brought to mind distant crowds, shouting orators, seas of banners.

Crushed in the doorway, Alice found herself aware for the first time in her life of a love so powerful she knew it could transform her. Echoing in her heart was the word spoken at the sight of her own nakedness – '*Beautiful*'.

Leo's masculine admiration for her body resonated in its turn in her own wonder at the sight of the naked men now uplifted, it seemed, and given a greater physical beauty by such a rich, engulfing ocean of sound. It was their hearts singing, she knew then, their hearts as well as their bodies, like hers transformed, peeled of etiquette, naked for everyone to see in a humble, human, perfect beauty. Love for the men and their singing consumed her so utterly she literally forgot where she was.

It took her a while to realize she was standing next to the medical orderly who had been operating so sensitively on the injured Japanese. He, like her, was absorbed by the singing. Although still dressed in his coat and cap, he had pulled down the mask usually worn over the nose and mouth. Head skewed awkwardly, she looked down at him. She knew he did not notice. It took her a few moments to overcome her astonishment and be sure about the round spectacles. She bent her head and whispered:

'*Bushido?*'

The eyes of Takeo-san slowly swivelled towards her.

9

The Chinese nurses chattered about distant dragons, saying day by day how much closer they were and how much louder and louder. Day by day the artillery exchanges grew fiercer. Full-scale Russian offensives were promised, followed, it was said, by imminent Japanese counterattacks, followed of course by imminent breaches of Russians defences, followed just as inevitably by unsustainably heavy Japanese losses, and so on, and so on. The sporadic booming prolonged itself into a barrage as loud as a monotonous thunder resounding peal on peal in the endless, icy, Manchurian wind.

All night long bright lights flashed beyond the shutters of Alice's bedroom. Shivering as much with cold as with fright, she sat up in bed clutching the bed covers to her chin and watched successive ghostly strips of light pattern the wall, glimmer in her dressing-table mirror, strike sparks from the silver picture frames of her great-grandmother and her parents and momentarily illumine them so that they seemed summoned for a moment into anxious, startled life.

Once or twice shells exploded so close the whole house shook. Crouched petrified in the darkness, she gave herself courage by thinking that the Mission was neutral. Gary Edstrom came round with a lantern to reassure her and offer alternative accommodation but she said she would prefer to stay in her own room even though the windows faced due south. In a while the distant flashes alarmed her hardly more than summer lightning. What kept her awake was the periodic, grating tinkle of a loose windowpane that never seemed to match the thunderous noise of gunfire but monitored its own version of events like a chirruping seismograph.

The chiming mechanism of the chapel clock had apparently been disrupted and she overslept. There was a banging on her door. She dressed in a hurry and went over to the ward where hot tea from the samovar revived her. Nurse Daisy and Francis Rawls were busy out in the reception area with the first casualties. The ground-floor ward itself was barely half full, most wounded having been evacuated to hospitals near the station. After tidying up, she sat in the white, antiseptic room and gazed periodically down at the brick floor or through the window at snowflakes tumbling like white confetti among the surrounding houses.

In the forefront of her mind were the dark silhouette of Leo in the doorway and, as if only to be expected, the sideways turned dark eyes of Takeo-san briefly smiling at her from behind their round lenses, only for him to vanish just as Leo had vanished and leave her with images of finality which she mistrusted but could not put out of her mind. Nagged though she was by anxieties, she knew she would never talk about either of them. Similarly she wondered about Izzy and Oliver, where they were now, who they were with. As for the score or so of men whose spontaneous singing had been so miraculous, most had gone. Other men's voices now began calling her.

She rose, did what they asked, comforted, knowing some by name, some by number, and in the process of looking after them her anxieties naturally lessened. Though the ward was only really warm where the stove was, she felt warmed by their companionship. There had been so many men to be nursed, men who were cooperative or resigned, fretful or friendly, most talkative, all against the war, all obliged to accept its inevitability. Now more were brought in by the masked, white-capped, white-coated orderlies either on stretchers or helped to hobble and, under Nurse Daisy's instructions, she calmed wherever possible, listened to the men's pleas and hoped to provide momentary relief and comfort against their pain and terror.

Then it was 'Help!' here and 'Help!' there and for days and nights she was literally rushed off her feet. The casualties were brought into the Mission by the score. Surrounding houses received the overflow. Francis Rawls collapsed with fatigue and Nurse Daisy for once allowed herself nips of vodka to keep her going. Despite the orders not to receive the seriously wounded, Alice found herself cutting away blood-sodden clothing to find blood-soaked and severed limbs and was unable to do more than patch up at best. Despite the way experience and competence had largely inured her to such sights and smells, she began to dread the arrival of each new cartload from across the Hun River.

One time, some days after the bombardment had started, she caught sight of her face in a mirror and did not immediately appreciate that the livid red streak below her right eye was blood from her own fingers and the discoloration of her hair was where she had stained it with her blood in trying to sweep it back beneath her bonnet. She looked down and saw the fresh crimson blood gleaming on her fingers as bright as the two rings she wore and remembered it must have come from a boy whose wounded shoulder she had just been tending. But Nurse Daisy had said with a shake of the head:

'It's no good, he's gone,' just like that, flat-voiced, and Alice had staggered into the little washroom off the ward and seen her face. It was as if she had been hit in the stomach, winded. She slumped into a wooden chair and stared at the wall with her mouth wide open.

'Hey,' called Nurse Daisy, 'there's someone here for you!'

Who on earth, Alice wondered, would want to see me now? She plunged her silk handkerchief with 'A' embroidered in one corner into a jug of water and dabbed at her face and hair. I am a sight, she thought. Who'd've thought I'd ever have done what I'm doing now or looked like I am now or not undressed for three or four nights and slept in the same clothes for three or four nights and be doing what I am doing now and not really be thinking any more whether or not they live or die?

'Yes?' she called back.

'There's a Russian gal here.'

'Who?'

'She says she's a nurse.'

Alice wiped away the last smear, took a final peek at herself in the mirror, noting only in the dim light of the little room that her complexion looked yellowish and drawn with tiredness, and went out into the ward again. One of the Chinese nurses answering that day to the name Lulu was standing beside two of the orderlies, and beside her was the nurse Arina. And leaning on Arina, the snow still thick on his fur hat and coat and riming an early growth of beard, was the stocky, strong figure of Leo. Nurse Daisy beckoned her over.

'Hey, it's the bad penny! Dr Leo's back!'

Alice saw Leo's face staring at her and Arina's bright pink face beside his. It did not register with her at once that *he* was there. In that instant he spoke in his good, almost unaccented English:

'I am here to help. Let me help…'

He seemed to sway as he spoke. Arina held him just in time. She said something rapidly in Russian that Alice did not fully understand but her addition of the English 'sick, very sick' was enough to make everyone, including Nurse Daisy, assist in helping him to a chair. He slumped into it and it was then that Alice saw the strain and illness in his features. Before there could be any explanation he tried to insist he would be all right despite Arina's saying that he had caught a fever.

'Boyo, you caught one peach of a fever, I'd say,' was Nurse Daisy's verdict. 'You need to be in the warm. Hey, Lulu, my dear, fetch therm-o-me-ter, chop-chop!'

No beds were free and in any case he refused to be treated as 'war wounded'. Placed near the stove and wrapped in a blanket, he shook uncontrollably with the fever. Through chattering teeth he gave Alice a broken account of his experience in the field stations after he had left Mukden. It took her a while, though she studied him closely, to believe the sunken eyes and blenched, thin, damp cheeks were his and not some stranger's. He had, of course, not really changed, but his strength had gone. Holding his hand, the grip was feeble. She could feel him trying to show his affection and gratitude through the handclasp and fail. Even the slight movement of his lips hardly suggested a smile.

'Alice, my darling...'

She wiped his face carefully with her 'Alice' handkerchief, the one he had given her after what she had done for Mr Wei's grandson.

'Don't,' she whispered. 'We don't need to talk. Later. I'm just glad...'

Arina said: 'I...I...' pointing at herself.

She had taken over, Alice thought. It was she who held the glass of sweet tea to his lips. Where she, Alice, should have helped, it was the bustling Arina who took charge of nursing Leo, but somehow it didn't seem to matter. Alice's eyes, turned from studying his face, strayed towards the faces of other men in the ward and then to the scene outside the window where dark clouds sidled past rumbling away like the guns and she recognised that Arina's was more than just a professional nursing interest. She probably loved him.

The thought occurred without a pang of bitterness. She had neither the inclination nor the time to be jealous. With Francis Rawls needing medical treatment himself and Nurse Daisy beginning to show signs of irritability through overwork, Alice was the one who had to make decisions. Since she was the one who now had the key, the Chinese staff looked to her to distribute fresh bandages and medical supplies from the storeroom. But so long as Leo was there it did not matter how hectic the work was. Each time she went past him, happy to see him sleeping, she felt her life had a focus.

Old Father Ambrosius and a younger priest, accompanied by a boy assistant, were as much in demand as she was. The reception area, the ward, the passages had all become filled up with supine or seated men, over which the nursing assistants and Russian medical orderlies and stretcher bearers had to step carefully. More and more Alice relied on the Chinese girls to clean and bandage the superficial wounds and offer mugs of tea. The advanced field stations, it turned out, were no longer working and all serious cases were being turned away. Men crossed themselves or sat motionless or groaned or smoked or suddenly began yelling with pain. The overcrowded ward had become filled with a dense odour of tobacco, sweat, damp clothing and the sharp scent of blood. The sight of the blood stained bandages and white-faced, bearded men was sickening. Possibly worse, though Alice had almost failed to notice it any more, was the constant underlying odour of urine, faeces and defeat.

Towards nightfall Gary Edstrom came over to see her. In a soft voice he announced that the ward would have to be closed.

'Why? Why?' she shouted back at him in a frantic, hurt, tired, resentful way.

He came accompanied by a group of Russian officers. They entered the ward with handkerchiefs to their noses, tiptoeing gingerly over outspread feet and looking at the men with a deadpan, rather haughty authority that instantly annoyed her. She was particularly annoyed that they had not been made to surrender their arms like the wounded. Their obviously full holsters attached to polished leather belts outside their greatcoats showed as much. Just as she started protesting a familiar voice stopped her.

'Veree delight-*ed*, Miss Alys-*a-a-a*! Ah, of *course*! Oliv-*er*, he tells me. You are in charge, yes?' It was Nikki Kozlov.

Tall and elegant in his spotless, well-cut greatcoat, he had lent himself an added, dandyish air by sporting an astrakhan hat worn at an absurdly precarious angle by comparison with the straight line of his moustache. Clean-shaven, he had a polished glow to his cheeks and jaw. On seeing her, he smiled broadly, his crystal eyes, unsettling as ever in their chestnut-brown sheen, seeming to glisten as he stepped forward, seized her hand, kissed it and clicked his heels.

'Tact-*icks*, my dear Miss Alys-*a-a-a*! Ah, but we *must*!'

'Tactics?'

'Retreat! We *must*!'

A shrug of the shoulders acknowledged that there were forces beyond his control. What could he do? The commander-in-chief, General Kuropatkin, had ordered a retreat. A Japanese army had been identified on the western flank of the Russian defence system and it threatened to sever the rail link with the north. All Russian soldiers were ordered to assemble near the station at Mukden in preparation for an orderly, tactical retirement to new positions north of the city.

'My dear, you *must pack*! All your *sings*! Every- *sing*! Now we ev-ac-u-*ate* all wound-*ed* men!'

Carts were apparently ready at the Mission entrance. She was surprised at such Russian efficiency, which had not been conspicuous before. It reduced her annoyance slightly to think that Nikki Kozlov now enjoyed a privileged position in the hierarchy of authority.

'Where is Oliver?'

Her question elicited a jerk from the straight of moustache.

'Oh, well, ver-*eee* well!'

'You're looking after him?'

'Why, of *course*! He will be 'elp-*ing*!'

'Helping?'

'Oh, yes! So now per-*mit* me, Miss Alys-*a-a-a*! I must leave. Pack every-*sing* you need, please!'

The salute was given with a simultaneous sharp forward bow, a friendly smile and a click of the heels. The instant he turned his back she knew she had no choice.

Leo was still asleep and she did not want to wake him. She went out into the Mission yard to go back to her room. Where earlier there had been distant flashes from the gunfire now the sky was lit by a vivid red glow. She remembered hearing that the retreating Russian columns had ignited their stores. Red gleams flickered pinkly in the blank glass of a few unshuttered windows and seemed to cast a halo of red over the silhouetted roofs.

The guns were so close their roar was deafening. It was said that the Japanese had brought up big-calibre Russian guns captured at Port Arthur. The ground was already littered with small nail-like fragments of metal and they crunched underfoot as she ran helter-skelter along the path to the house.

In the hallway she saw the two terrified Chinese girls. She asked about Elizabeth. 'No Missy,' they said, 'no Missy,' or that is what she thought they said, and Elizabeth's room – Uncle Elliott's former room - was in fact empty. Where was she? They didn't know. Alice dashed to her bedroom.

The two girls stood and watched her. Intermittently lights flashed beyond the River Hun and the bedroom was lit up starkly. When it wasn't, there was the eerie red glow suggesting a brilliant sunset that made the shadows seem deep as water risen to window-level around the furniture. Alice had a sense of wading as she moved from bed to wardrobe to dressing table stuffing things quickly into her suitcase. She could not do it quickly enough. Everything rattled as the shells fell closer, not just the windowpane. Little cascades of shrapnel would run down the roof with the menacing pitter-patter of rats' feet.

Yes, she was going, she told the girls. She was going away with the Russians. They bowed to her. Have I the faintest idea what I am really doing? As she thought this she picked up the silver photograph frames. It was as if she had never gone anywhere without having at the back of her mind the idea that this was merely a stopover and she might leave at any moment. The thought held her mesmerised for quite a while despite knowing she should hurry as much as possible and when she emerged from the daydream she quickly shook herself and pressed whatever was surplus to her needs into the girls' hands. They bowed and thanked her. She pulled on her leather overcoat and picked up the suitcase. Would she not come back? They asked.

'I don't know. Perhaps…'

On the point of leaving the bedroom, she heard voices outside the house. Her first thought was that someone had been hurt by falling debris. Then she heard her own name being called and pushed past the Chinese girls to come immediately face to face with Lulu, the Chinese nurse, followed by Oliver. She was astonished to see him. Where had he come from? How was he? He looked distressed. He had come with 'old Kozzer', he said. He fought his stammer.

'Alice…'

'What?'

Again he fought it. 'D-D-Dr L-L-Leo…'

'What?'

'…h-h-hurt!'

'What do you mean?'

'A s-s-soldier with a b-b-bayonet…'

'What?'

'The s-s-soldier…b-b-bayonet…'

He gave a kind of demonstration as he forced the words out of his mouth. She stared at him. Her first reaction was a wish not to know, a wish not to understand. Then he seized her by one arm and picked up her suitcase with the other.

Before she could put two words together she was being rushed back to the hospital wing. The red glow now flared up and died down. She smelled burning in the air close at hand. A wind blew full of a light, stinging grit. As she ran, Alice had the feeling that it was not happening to her, could not be happening. *This* was not real, something else happening somewhere else was real. The news about Leo could not be real and she could not be running breathlessly now on the heels of the agile Chinese nurse who bobbed up and down ahead of her, the wings of her headdress flying out whitely either side of her.

In the ward it turned out to be true. During the evacuation a wounded man had apparently gone berserk. He had attacked one of the Russian orderlies with a bayonet, killing him. Then he had attacked a second and caused severe wounds. Leo had sprung to the orderly's aid and in the struggle his left hand had been badly cut.

The ward was empty save for the detritus of soiled bedclothes and mattresses. The Chinese staff were clearing up. Leo had apparently been moved into the reception area. She discovered him there being attended by Arina who had applied a tourniquet and was doing her best to staunch the bleeding and clean the wound.

So far as Alice could tell, the palm of his left hand had received a deep, lateral cut. Unwilling as he was to show her the wound, his eyes closed against the pain, she forced herself to look closely. A wave of nausea rose through her at the sight and she felt herself becoming unsteady. Meanwhile he was gripping his left wrist with his right hand, drawing in quick, rasping breaths.

Alice knew that Arina would have liked to take charge, but even she looked scared. The sole illumination in the reception area was provided by two large oil lamps suspended from the ceiling. They shed adequate light normally, but suddenly they were extinguished by a violent explosion just beside the Mission building. In the split instant of it happening, before the sound of the explosion actually reached her, Alice distinctly saw the panes of glass appear to be sucked outwards, instinctively lowered her head and then, with the sound bursting on her in ear-splitting thunder, heard a fierce whistling of flying glass as the whole window was blown in and the lights went out. In a moment she had fingers to her forehead and felt blood.

It did not mean anything to her at first. She could not be sure either of the blood on her fingers or the oval eyes looking at her through round lenses. Was she in a daydream again? Was it possible that now, in the half-light of a sort of lantern he carried with him, she was dreaming about his eyes being close to hers and smiling at her? That he should be smiling while the white curtains billowed behind him into the room through the smashed window made it seem he possessed angel's wings in addition to his white coat and mask. The fact slowly broke through the improbabilities of her shocked state. The sound of broken glass crackling under his feet reinforced the reality. He *was* there, she recognised, and her momentary speculation about whether or not he should be glad that one of his own Japanese shells had caused the damage, or whether he should be considered their enemy, was dispelled the very same instant by the sight of the recognition showing clearly in his eyes when he saw Leo. He peered into Leo's face and then looked down at the wound and shook his head, gave a hissing sound, pondered a moment, nodded, then whispered:

'Good! Good!'

Both Lulu and Arina had gone and whatever more he may have said was drowned by someone laughing hysterically out in the Mission yard and several voices calling to each other frantically in the darkness of the passageway. Alice heard feet running out of the Mission entrance. She half-heartedly wiped away the blood from her forehead with her handkerchief, concentrating all the time on watching Leo's reaction and hearing the amazement in his voice.

'Not, no, it cannot be! Takeo-san, is it you?'

'Please, good flend...'

The curtains were flapping about. Leo bared his teeth in a contorted grin.

'It is! Yellow Peril – it is!'

'Yellow Pellil, oh, yes! Dr Leo, you badly hurt, yes?'

'What is Takeo-san doing here?'

'Please, no move, no talk…'

To Alice's eyes he was behaving in the oddest way. Instead of dealing with Leo's hand he started drawing his coat collar away from his neck.

'No move, please. I wish to cut…'

His voice was sharp, resonant and authoritative. He went on speaking as he worked quickly, cutting away part of Leo's collar with sharp scissors and appearing to disregard his injured hand completely. In his odd staccato English he confessed he had seen Leo in the ward and recognised him, but did not want to show he did.

'Alysa-Amerikanka, she knows who I am.'

He said it not so much directly to her as to himself as he bared Leo's shoulder and undid the tourniquet. The paleness of the curve of the shoulder against the darkness created for Alice an image of terrible vulnerability and, overwhelmed by an urge to protect, she rushed to Leo, only for the little man's eyes to give a warning flash of defiance and deter her. With rapid, practised movements he was fixing little steel needles into Leo's neck, down his shoulder and his upper arm. When she protested slightly, all he did was signal for her to hold the lantern up so he could see exactly where to insert them. She obeyed, daunted by an authority exercised without his hardly saying a word. It appeared Leo could open his hand fully now.

'I never taught you it.'

He spoke laconically and a little shakily.

Takeo-san chuckled. 'No, it is China medicine. Velly clever, velly good.'

It amazed Alice how quickly the bleeding was reduced to the point where it was possible to clean the wound and prepare it for suturing. This Takeo-san did carefully, using a curved needle and material which he unwound from a little envelope.

'How?' she asked. 'Takeo-san, how?'

His concentration was so great he did not look up. She was in any case riveted by the sight of his brisk fingers working on the wound with the quickness of a sewing-machine needle. Looking into Leo's face, she saw an amazement matching her own. Ruefully he smiled back at her and winked. Neither spoke. Silence seemed the only adequate response to such dexterity.

A clangour of metal grinding on stone, the rattle of wagons, horses' hooves, voices shouting, the frou-frou of a passing army could be heard outside. Feet tramped or ran by and there was a creaking of cart wheels. So preoccupied was Alice by alternately watching the quick, dancing fingers and holding up the lantern to see Leo's face that she scarcely noticed noises from elsewhere. She did not even wonder where Arina or the Chinese nurses had gone. It was only the sharp little rifle-fire of feet running through broken glass that broke her concentration. She looked up to see Nurse Daisy come rushing in, announcing that she had been in the upper ward when the shell exploded.

'Hey, your poor face! You're all covered in blood!'

'What?'

'Didn't you know?'

'Blood!'

Alice was first made properly conscious of it by that exclamation. The blood had run down her cheek. She dared not think what had happened to her, except that feeling the wetness on her temples and cheeks took away the last vestiges of her strength. Nausea and shivering quickly forced her to relinquish the lantern into Leo's free hand and sink into a chair. Nurse Daisy was saying what a blessing it was that none of the glass had got in her eyes. No, the glass cuts were limited to her temples, she said. Alice succumbed limply to the efficient but hurtful nursing care, the inevitable stinging pain of iodine dabbed on her cuts and the news that another shell had landed near the Mission cemetery, damaged the roof of the school building and started a fire in a kerosene store. Gary Edstrom was apparently organising efforts to extinguish it.

'They're near the Hun River, the Japs,' said Nurse Daisy. 'They'll be here tomorrow or the day after.'

The implication of her words was amply borne out by the noise from beyond the smashed windows. Urgent shouted commands mingled with the wind's continuous whistling and the rustle of the curtains served as overtures to the larger thunderous roar of a giant movement, a solid lava flow of tramping feet and creaking wheels and whinnying horses and a recognition, perceptible but unspoken, that this sound now overlay and largely replaced the endless gunfire of recent days.

Suddenly Gary Edstrom entered the reception area followed by Elizabeth, his face in the poor light marked by harlequin-like smears of black soot.

'The windows are out, is that it? Anyone hurt?'

The question was redundant since it was obvious that both Alice and Leo were receiving attention. Elizabeth raced to her, too out of breath, it seemed, to say anything before Gary, seeing her, started making an announcement.

'Everyone, please listen. I've got to say this. God is with you, I know that in my soul, but the Mission… the Mission must be neutral. I am sorry, I cannot guarantee the safety of anyone who is not a citizen of the United States. I must ask anyone who is not a citizen of the United States of America to…'

His voice stopped. Alice suddenly found Elizabeth's arms round her. Although she was sitting and Nurse Daisy was struggling to tie the bandage, Elizabeth still hugged her. Otherwise the only sound in the room was the crackling of glass as Gary Edstrom shifted his weight from foot to foot.

'… I have to ask them to leave. The Mission must remain neutral, you see. We have to assume there will be a new administration here shortly and… and times will have changed. In the light of that we must ensure we are neutral.'

It was strange that nobody spoke. The words had that effect. No one was safe. The air blown in from outside, no matter how chilly, had an acrid, burnt smell, just as the noise of the retreating army filled the darkness with a sort of spreading contamination of the very idea that the Mission could remain a sanctuary. Alice looked up into Elizabeth's face and felt this was the end. She was one of the defeated. She knew in her heart that she would choose the lung-searing sharpness of the icy outer air rather than the hospital miasma of her recent life.

'There,' Nurse Daisy said, fixing a safety pin in place.

'I am going, Elizabeth dear,' Alice whispered.

'Stay, stay, stay! Be our guardian again! Stay, please!'

'No, I can't!'

'Oh, but you must!' Elizabeth's eyebrows, puckering with emotion, formed twin demanding arcs at that point, until she was suddenly overtaken by another thought. 'Oh, I forgot…Look, this came for you. I don't know how it got here but we think it must be for you.'

Alice felt some paper being thrust into her hand. She screwed up her eyes to look at it but all she could discern was a grubby envelope. Hardly less unexpected than the almost indecipherable series of forwarding addresses on the front and Alice's cry of 'Oh, it's from my father!' was Elizabeth's urgent renewal of her whispered effort of persuasion.

'Can't you just stay a short while? You see, it's our secret…'

'What's your secret?'

'We're going to get married.'

'Oh, I'm so glad for you!'

'But we're keeping it a secret. I just wanted you to know.'

Elizabeth kissed her. Alice hugged the girl to her. Yet over her shoulder she caught sight of Leo, his hand now bandaged. He had obviously been looking across at the two of them and when his and Alice's eyes met he winked once again.

'Oh, I'm sure you'll be happy.' She spoke sincerely and simply and with complete confidence. 'Of course, you know who's here, don't you?'

'Who?'

'Oliver.'

Alice nodded towards him. He had just appeared in the doorway carrying Alice's suitcase. At the moment of recognition Elizabeth opened her mouth to greet him and even uttered his name, but in the little interval between recognition and remonstrance she did not even have time to rush to him before he had come across and seized her in his arms. He had apparently been helping to extinguish the fire in the kerosene store, as his smudged face bore witness. His arrival had coincided with another. Vassia was there in the doorway, waving.

'*Poshl-e-e-e!*' his gruff voice shouted. 'Come! Come! Go home! *Domoi! Domoi!*'

'God bless you one and all!' cried Gary Edstrom. 'Yes, God bless you all! I'm sorry, I can't promise you'll be safe here. So God be with you! God be with you!'

10

'*Vy kogo-zhe znaete?*'
'*Znaiu. Poka bolshe ne skazhu.*'
'*Nu, Vassia, molodets ty!*'

The cart swayed. Vassia had managed to obtain a cart and an animal to pull it. They swayed through the eastern gate into Mukden and, as if a shutter had fallen, the gritty, icy, snow-filled wind dropt almost to nothing.

Ahead and behind them the slow, uneven footfalls of marching men, the creak of cartwheels, neighing, shouts, distant gunfire filled otherwise silent and virtually deserted streets already permeated by faint gusts of smoke-tainted air. Few Chinese dared watch.

After the usual noise of the busy city even the occasional barking of dogs from the darkened mass of buildings seemed merely to sharpen the sense of emptiness for Alice, perched up as she was on the gently swaying cart as if sailing on a dark sea, with Leo pressed tightly beside her under thick blankets drawn over their shoulders. While Vassia drove, Takeo-san sat with them in the back of the cart, disguised by his cap and facemask, with a parka clutched round him and the hood over his head, posing no threat to their safety now, Alice supposed, whatever threat he might have posed to Russian fortunes while he had been at the Mission. Resting under his feet was her suitcase.

Seeing her white bandages and the Red Cross band on her arm, men crossed themselves and bowed both to her and the little entourage of Arina, walking behind them, still in her nurse's wimple, and Oliver, beside her, now wearing a Russian army greatcoat and cap with earflaps. Urgency dogged them. Military discipline had obviously been replaced by the discipline of shared misfortune. Men reluctant to go any further reeled about drunk, sat and stared, dozed or smoked while officers, some mounted, kept order in a desultory way, brandishing guns and riding whips. To Alice's eyes the common despair at surrendering Mukden was outweighed by the fact that troops at the limits of their endurance knew their last enemy was not the Japanese but the Manchurian winter. No one would chivvy them into facing it. No bugles would entice or spur them, she thought. They would retreat stubbornly into it in their own good time.

The western gateway was crowded. Remembering the first time she walked through it with Mr Wei and how the Chinese had stood to one side as the Russian convoy dashed past, she watched now as men drifted through in irregular lines. It was as if the sheer force of the howling wind sucked them out one by one. Under the discipline of its shrill icy parade-ground voice they leant into the darkness, stooped, anonymous, a stream of snow-dusted hats, shoulders, swaying rifles and bobbing bayonets stretching as far ahead of her as she could see beneath telegraph lines and the distant spasmodic glow from the station. The instant the cart went through the gate, up flapped the blanket. She had to fight to keep it round her, just as she had to struggle to keep her place beside Leo as Vassia pulled sharply on the reins. Ahead, dimly, more lights turned out to be fires lit beside the railway line north of the station. They headed in that direction.

'If... if you have...'

It was Vassia speaking over his shoulder in Russian. He passed them a vodka bottle. The remark made Leo laugh.

'What?'

She saw Leo's face in profile. It was about all she saw clearly through the snow.

'You know what Kuropatkin means?'

'No.'

'Partridge. Partridges always fly from guns. So if you have partridges as generals, eh?'

The gritty, dusty wind sprang up and died down, then again flicked snow in their faces.

'They fly from guns – naturally.'

She laughed. They each took nips of vodka.

'*Na zdorovie!* We fly from guns.'

Leo's voice was husky but quite audible beside her ear. She gulped the vodka and felt it race through her stomach like fire. Its effect was suddenly matched by an explosion close at hand. She started shaking and clung to him.

'Ours,' he assured her quietly.

An answering shell whistled overhead and burst somewhere far beyond the embankment. The animal panicked and made the cart shake so violently it almost tipped them out. Leo's right arm round her shoulders held her tight.

This, the strength of his right arm, was the only reassurance she needed. The physicality of the protectiveness seemed so enclosing it comforted and stimulated her like a passionate kiss. Despite the nagging, spasmodic pain of her own cuts she sought the lure of his closeness. It was masculine, sexual, and it made her lean into him in a way she knew could seem wanton and lascivious, yet it was just such a wantonness she felt and longed for with the hunger of long abstinence. Fighting against it, as if her body were filled with a wild sea of fiercely contrary currents and tides, was love not as passion but as concern, as a desperate wish to comfort, to be needed by him as exclusively as she needed him. What she fought against, as he held his bandaged left hand close to his chest, was the knowledge that the pain, like the shell-shock deafness, choked off close contact, just as she tried to prevent him from knowing how much each jolt of the cart, so sharp and sudden in the darkness, sharpened the pain of her cuts.

Alongside the railway track, with the low embankment and the earth rampart offering a windbreak, fires had been lit and mobile kitchens set up. Round them men crowded and squatted, spooning up the hot stew. Here, the instant they were helped down from the cart, Leo and Alice squatted with them and enjoyed the hot food.

Hundreds of anonymous, grey-coated men, almost silent in the momentary contentment of eating and enjoying the temporary warmth, seemed to her to obliterate fear, or at least she was so cheered by their presence she felt caught up in a shared fear that dwarfed her single fear and made it irrelevant. The light from the fires silhouetted the figures standing or squatting, the rifles and bayonets stacked upright like stooks of corn and the storm of grit and snow blowing over it all with the force of a bellows making the flames flare up, illumine their surroundings for a moment or so, then sink into a steady gleam. The effect created an odd, unreal sense of being at home and safe.

Oliver and Arina squatted together near her. His bright eyes, showing their whites as he glanced sideways at the girl, were unaware of Alice watching and Arina, looking from time to time towards Leo, seemed deliberately neglectful until she responded between spoonfuls by smiling at Oliver with surprising tenderness. For Alice this very tenderness seemed to her a guarantee that her own fondness for Oliver had been replaced and enhanced by another, though she knew in her heart the girl's care was more fraternal than truly loving.

'Kuropatkin,' Leo whispered.

'Kuropatkin?'

She recognised then a tautening of the atmosphere among the men. A bright beam of light swept through the darkness of the embankment above them, followed by smoke churning in whitish, wind-blown clouds from the stack of a locomotive coming into view like a dragon out of Mukden station.

Spontaneously, as it rolled slowly by, a kind of groan rose. No more than slits of light showed either side of drawn blinds in the windows. Armed guards were posted fore and aft on the outer platforms of the carriages.

'What's it mean?' Alice asked.

'It means our general is leaving. Fleeing from guns.'

'You mean the war's over?'

He smiled feebly. 'Our war is over, yes.'

At that moment Oliver sprang to his feet with an urgent cry. 'We must be going, too! Vassia said he'd find us places. On one of the trains,'

There was a general movement among the men, but he paused, anticipating Alice's reaction. All she did was glance up at him.

'I'm staying.'

He understood enough to reassure her.

'We'll come back for you. You s-s-stay here!'

In a moment he and Arina had gone, before Alice had time to notice how, like heavy birds rising reluctantly flight after flight in ragged order, men were clambering up, stamping their feet, collecting their baggage and weapons, beginning to move off. She felt an instantaneous wave of panic at the thought of being left behind. But Leo on one side of her did not stir and it was only then she realized that Takeo-san was on his far side, rocking gently to and fro as he squatted facing the fire.

'Why did we come here?'

Leo asked the question very quietly and angrily through gritted teeth. In the flicker of the flames she tried to persuade herself that the pallor of his skin, even the greyness of his lips and the way his eyes seemed to recede into bruised hollows, were symptoms simply of fatigue, the same fatigue afflicting her. For that reason she was happy to spend a few more moments within the circle of warmth from the fire. Chinese had come out of their houses and were gathered along the rampart. Rows of faint yellow faces now watched the coming and going, the arms being stacked as more men came from Mukden, the lines forming before kitchens and, over it all, the snowy, flame-licked darkness.

'I came because of you,' Alice whispered. She saw his mouth curve in a smile.

A gun carriage creaked by just beyond the fire. Steam flew about from the mobile kitchens. A new red glow had developed just south of the station and semaphored through the darkness.

'I came to satisfy my warlords and to escape my past.' Leo was talking partly to himself, partly to the rosy, fire-warmed, gusty air, partly as if the words were emerging from a dream. He placed an arm round Alice's shoulders. 'No, no, let me just, you know, talk and talk like all Russians. We Russians love talk. Yes, it is time to talk now, to talk perhaps to ourselves because we are never exactly today who we were or are going to be who we are. You see, I was never one person. I was always doctor and surgeon and man of ideals.' A shake of the head and a short laugh. 'I hoped to change society. I wished to help poor people. I was member of our intelligentsia. And because... because of it, changing this, changing that, I changed my name and I almost – almost – lost myself. I became your name.' The arm round her shoulders tightened as Leo's voice became firmer. 'I have to say I was wrong. Now I know it is no good. Oh, yes it is beautiful, full of... full of beautiful pretensions to goodness and love of humanity. But it also takes away... takes away what is very precious. It takes away what is personal and what you call private life. It takes away...'

She could not hear what he was saying because men started shouting nearby as a further train approached very slowly. This time cattle trucks with open doors slowly rolled past one by one and in a hubbub of swearing and cries men hurled down their weapons as they scrambled to climb aboard, sometimes helped up, sometimes forced back either by those already inside or by attempts to keep order.

She wondered if they should try to get aboard as well, but the arm round her shoulders held her close. Whatever Leo was saying, because he went on speaking into the darkness despite the noise, kept her beside him. She thought she heard him talk about love and keeping faith, words that became a reminder to her of her own need to keep faith with her heritage. To be free, after all, could only have real meaning if it were blessed with gratitude for release and become renewal. For her the renewal meant defiance.

What her Granny Luke had once spoken of came back to her, the massa and missus heritage she had known as a child, and how she, her mother's mother, had remembered seeing the men and women working in the sugar canes all day long. That was what came back to her suddenly in response to Leo's confession that he was never one person. She, Alice May, shivered, knowing there had always been the servile other, if personified only in the nameless, yellowing photograph of Granny Luke's mother, her great-grandmother, that she had kept with her in a silver frame. She was the ghost from Jamaican slavery, anonymous, it seems, whose name had never been mentioned by either Granny Luke herself or Alice's mother and whose photograph labelled 'Grandmother' had only come to light among her mother's things after her death. Indeed, the Negro features were the only clue to identity. It would be a betrayal of her heritage to deny that truth, but she knew that to assert it would need a gathering defiance much like the sort of air around her so full of the men stirred into movement, their features sculpted momentarily out of the red rock of the darkness.

Leo was saying something. 'It takes away what Miss Maddocks said. She said...'

Alice could not hear exactly. He was still talking about keeping

promises, it seemed, being oneself, being faithful. Because that was the truth.
The truth.
'I am born free - *freeborn*! That's the truth!'
It was her cry. It bit into the darkness as into Leo's talk.

Takeo-san heard it. He had seemed so impassive that Alice could not be sure he had heard anything and it took her a little by surprise to see him draw the mask away from his nose and mouth and slowly remove his spectacles. The young-looking features dissolved spontaneously into the puckerings and wrinkles of an odd little smile.

'Ah, fleedom! I also, honolable lady, my flend, I, Yellow Pellil, must say this. I serve my county, yes.' He continued swaying as he spoke. 'I serve my county, but I also am not honolable person. Fleedom, that is what I want. To be like you, honolable lady, to be *free-born*, that is what I want. Not to be slave! If I serve I am not free. So... So to be honolable person is not possible any more for me, not possible in my county.'

They waited for him to say more, but he appeared to have become distracted by throwing a piece of wood on the fire. The sparks and flames scattered hissing in the wind.

'First thing is wish to be better, wish to implove. Wish to be good person. Wish to be good surgeon and better surgeon. Second thing is... fleedom. I wish fleedom now, only fleedom. End of war, peace... and fleedom.' He swayed again, giving the impression of being rocked by the gusts of wind. 'Mostly... mostly I wish fleedom to be... to be plivate. Wish to be plivate person.'

Having said this, he replaced his round spectacles and his facemask and the disguise of the parka pulled over his head.

'Amen,' said Leo quietly. He turned to Alice. 'Why freeborn?'
'My great-grandmother was a slave. In Jamaica.'
'My grandfather – no, my great-grandfather, he was serf.'
'So?'
'We are...'
'Similar?'
'Yes, similar.' He laughed. 'So where is freedom now?'
'Where?'

The pressure of his arm round her caused a rustling of paper in her pocket.

'I must go home,' she said immediately. 'America. That'll be...'

She had disliked it for a while, the America her mother hated because of her father's disloyalty. Now she knew it would be literally a new world with Leo there and Takeo-san joining them. In any case, it was the only link. She had to be certain that one place was her home, her hope of freedom. As if to reassure herself she licked her lips and spoke out boldly.

'I have had this letter and some money. My father is waiting for me there. I was on my way there when I came here. Now you will come with me. Both of you, won't you? It'll be *our* home. You'll be free.'

Leo's arm squeezed her.

'Of course! Of course we go! To America! We go to America!'

11

Oliver ran out of the darkness into the circle of the firelight. Seats, he said breathlessly in a low voice for fear of being overheard, seats. A last train was leaving and seats were allocated.

They went from fire to fire alongside the low embankment. It surprised and comforted Alice that Leo, though still weak and in need of her help, coped so well in face of the need to hurry, especially as explosions had begun to occur from time to time where the night sky shone red. Above them, on the embankment, a train lumbered by. Tarpaulin-draped barrels of field artillery on flat wagons tapped their way in slow procession over rails bowing gently under each load. Guards silhouetted beside the weapons appeared faceless and sombre but did not prevent men rushing in droves towards the slow-moving wagons, driven by waves of panic, shouting, struggling to achieve a foothold, being pushed back, struggling again and in the melee shoving Alice and Leo this way and that.

Scarcely able to keep on her feet as she tried to follow Oliver, she was glad to be led up a slight incline into an empty, exposed area of sidings. Seeing little apart from the shape of Oliver ahead of her, she held Leo firmly by the arm and tried to shade her eyes from the stinging grit of the snow while stumbling over rails and sleepers which bright flashes from the south lit up instant by instant. Oliver said it was all right, they were ammunition dumps. In their wake came the delayed, hollow, cumulative thunder of explosions. She glimpsed sparks of light struck from Takeo-san's spectacle lenses as he helped Leo on the other side and heard him muttering 'Not guns, not guns, we safe, we safe!'

Beckoning and calling, having seized Alice's suitcase from her, Oliver skipped ahead of them towards what in the darkness looked like a sheer cliff face. Gradually it became distinguishable through the eye-watering mixture of snow and dust as a barracks building. Beside it loomed a locomotive, unlit save for the bright firebox glow in the cabin. Beyond it were crowds of people, some civilian, some military, so far as she could see, milling around in the darkness.

Alice felt so exhausted by the effort of running and stumbling she could hardly bring herself to push her way through and was relieved when Vassia suddenly emerged from the press of people and almost picked Leo up bodily to convey him towards a carriage.

Oliver shouted in her ear that it was the last train. He urged her to climb aboard.

'Please, Alice, there are s-s-seats!'

'I don't care!' she suddenly cried at him.

She did not know why she behaved like that. The crowds round her seemed to squeeze the breath out of her and leave her with a sense of drowning. In her desperation all she wanted was to struggle free. She fought against one body after another and was gradually thrust backwards, away from the train. Eager to draw breath, even to rest a moment, she was pushed back towards the high fence separating the barracks from the railway track.

It was her private panic, she knew. Crowds had always been a source of terror. Now, in the darkness filled with snow and vague shapes, she felt she had entered one of her infrequent but hideous nightmares from which she could only emerge by literally using will power to stop the force of the nightmare taking hold. Finding herself by a gateway, she leaned against the gatepost and breathed in deep lungfuls of icy air. Grateful for the chance to rest, she felt her heart beating madly. Then something caught her eye.

Bayonets glinted in what appeared to be a cordon of soldiers lined up beneath the huge lightless elevation of the barracks. She peered through the blizzard of white dots of snow and saw other patches of white. The guards had cordoned off groups of men, she realized. Some wore white head bandages; some had their arm in white slings. At first she assumed they were being protected. They would be allowed to get on the train later, she supposed. Unable to hear what exactly was being shouted, she thought she recognised some of the very men she might have seen earlier that day at the Mission and noticed they were waving, not merely to attract her attention but signalling for some reason, as if they wanted her to go farther down the line of the fence, wanted her to see what was happening farther down the length of the train. She assumed this from their gestures and waved back tentatively, mistrustful of her own senses and the nightmarish terror from which she had been trying to escape. The nightmare receded slightly through this act of recognition. Though she knew it would probably be impossible to get closer to them because of the cordon, not to mention the surrounding noise and snow, she felt they would not have signalled so urgently unless they really wanted her help. So she began quickly making her way as best she could through the crowd, past the first carriage and the second, and into a darker area of cattle wagons with steeply pitched roofs.

At once she understood. Ramps were down and horses were being driven up into the wagons. They came through a second gateway and were being herded rather than led because the explosions, growing fiercer almost by the second, made it hard to control them. Handlers on either side of each horse strained at taut ropes, pulled and goaded them to mount the ramps while officers swore at them. No matter how strenuously the handlers tried to hold them, the horses were seized by a common terror that no amount of beating could overcome and reared and kicked out and plunged about in the dark with reddened, maddened eyes. Their antics blocked the gateway and stopped access to the train.

It also stopped her. She strained her eyes to see through the murk of the deeper darkness what was happening by the barracks building and made out a man on crutches. Suddenly lit up by a brightening of the night followed by a further loud explosion, he was waving. Perhaps he was shouting as well but she could not hear. What the instant of brightness showed was that he was one of dozens, it seemed, waving at her from beyond the silhouetted shapes of guards cordoning them. Equally, as if all other noise had abated a moment, the noise of frantically clattering hooves and shouts and neighing and officers' whistles yielded to the faint sound of voices chanting.

'*Amerika-a-anka! Pomog-i-i-te! Amerika-a-anka! Amerika-a-anka!* '

It came in a wave and was gone. Even her own name, she thought, came within earshot for an instant. Then the immediately surrounding uproar obliterated it.

She was being asked to help, was that it? Why? What was she meant to do?

Peering again, she saw farther back in the darkness that other ghostly shapes came into view. There were rows of carts lined up nose to tail, some with the shafts stuck up in the air. The waving and the gestures from the shapes beyond the cordon seemed to grow more insistent.

She ran through the gateway despite the rearing horses and shouts of warning. Though teeming snowflakes made it hard for her to see, she rushed impulsively towards the cordon and glimpsed enough to know that the carts were filled with wounded men. In other groups stood the less severely wounded with their blood stained bandages. They were *her* men, she was certain, men she had seen at the Mission, she thought, calling at her and waving but separated from her partly by the armed guards and partly by horses that had broken free of their handlers.

It was all she needed to know. The wounded, *her* wounded, were being sacrificed for the sake of the cavalry! They would be left behind by the last train out of Mukden!

Suddenly a determination became fixed in her mind. She at least would not leave without them, nor, she imagined, would Leo, if he knew, but it was all up to her now and she would do now what she had to do.

The guards forming the cordon were clearly in two minds by this time. One of the horses terrified by the last spate of explosions had just charged down and badly injured a couple of them. They had been dragged towards the fence on the instructions of officers but all attempts to chivvy the other men back into line had been met by a surly reluctance to obey and a concerted beating of hands into armpits against the cold. Alice saw her chance. She hurried back to the gateway and confronted the officer most obviously in charge of the attempted embarkation. Scared eyes blinked back at her out of a young beardless face. The sudden realization of his fright gave her a fierce renewal of determination.

'What are you doing?' she cried.

Her shrill voice had a surprising sharpness and clarity despite the surrounding uproar. Another officer came rushing up with a drawn revolver, shouting something to his younger colleague. Rudely he tried to push her away.

'These are wounded men!' she shouted in his face.

He looked astonished.

'Get them on the train!' she shouted.

Her pointing at the train and the sharp stridency of her voice brought up other officers.

'They should be on the train!' she shouted. 'On the train!'

A chorus of frantic cries now broke out from the wounded men beyond the cordon. It rose to a spontaneous crescendo and could be heard above all the shouting and commotion of the horses and their handlers. A flow of invective poured from one officer's lips as he pushed Alice back. The shoving incensed her. She shrieked out:

'Why horses? Why not *your* wounded? Why?'

She did not know how she managed to make herself heard. Some piercing quality in her cries perhaps or the very force of her indignation or the way she shouted in English or the blood stained whiteness of Nurse Daisy's bandage, worn almost like a badge of authority, compelled attention. All she knew was that such an explosion of anger had occurred inside her it brought redoubled strength to her shouts. There was also the fact that the maddened horses and the collapsing discipline worked in her favour. She was instantly surrounded by a small crowd. The officer's attempt to seize her arm led her to struggle against him so vigorously several men came to her aid. She managed to break free and run back through the gateway.

The first thing she did was to seize hold of the nearest cart. Pulling at the upturned shafts as hard as she could, she started dragging the cart free from the one behind it. The action puzzled the wounded and the orderlies standing nearby until they realized what she was doing. There was an instantaneous reversal of the previous state of things. All the earlier discipline now snapped.

Galvanised, the guards and orderlies and others followed her example. They joined her in pulling other carts towards the wagons.

The sight of carts two abreast laden with wounded men being rushed through the gateway caused a stampede among the horses. Disarray and panic quickly overwhelmed the handlers. Simultaneous explosions, so loud this time the earth literally seemed to tremble, forced even the strongest men to let go of the straining animals. A mounted officer in jodhpurs and gleaming brown boots tried to re-impose authority, reared up his horse, drew a revolver and fired several shots. Immediately one of the guards crumpled and fell. A wave of shock reinforced the general sense of outrage and helped to focus it. Even the horse handlers now changed sides. They began driving the horses from the wagons. Alice, helped by half-a-dozen others, mostly medical orderlies, pulled her cart towards one of the ramps and watched appalled as the officer was dragged off his mount, knocked to the ground and trampled beneath their hooves by fleeing horses.

Her action led to a frenzied assault on the recently emptied wagons. Dozens of carts were pulled and pushed, often too unceremoniously for some of the wretched wounded. Their yells of pain mingled with the shouts of the able-bodied men who seized the carts and lifted them up over the ridges on the ramps and carried them swaying into the wagons' interiors. There seemed to be no need for supervision at this point. All were seized by a fever of purposeful activity that disregarded any attempt to countermand it. The wounded should have priority, that was obvious. By the score they were either carried up the ramps or assisted to hobble. The carts themselves, once they had served their purpose, were either flung out on the adjacent rails or left standing in a jumble at the points where the ramps of the full wagons had been raised. No one was to be left behind. Alice saw to that. She ran frantically to and fro directing new cartloads to wherever space was available. And one after another the wagons, already laid with millet straw for the horses, were transformed into makeshift wards for the men she regarded as *her* wounded.

Shrill whistles sounded. The bell on the locomotive rang out. Then voices started shouting it was a ruse to stop more wounded being brought up. The ploy worked only for a moment. The train jerked forward, but an absolute frenzy of yelling and screaming brought it to a halt. To the accompaniment of cheers and shouts and renewed lowering of ramps, more carts were rushed up and wounded were lifted aboard while horses neighed wildly somewhere out of sight and occasionally dashed towards the activity round the wagons, only to shy away again as soon as another explosion occurred. Alice, anxious for the animals as much as for the wounded, was relieved to see that several handlers had begun to round them up. Many, it seemed, had been saddled and ridden off.

'Miss May! Miss May! You know it is ag-*ainst* ord-*ers*!'

Nikki Kozlov startled her as he came out of the darkness. His voice had grown so high-pitched it sounded almost feminine. He looked far less spruce than when she had last seen him. His astrakhan hat may have been worn at a jaunty angle, but he had dirt marks on his cheeks and temples and his eyes glittered with a mixture of panic and despair.

'Our commander-in-*chief*,' he shrieked. Men buffeted him as he spoke. They were either bringing up more carts or rushing to save their skins. He uttered sharp, fragmentary cries.

'General Kuropatkin … strict ord-*ers*!… Hors-*es*!… Caval-*ree*!… must *dee*-fend!… Miss May! Dear Miss May, what are you *doo*-ing?'

The whistling and bell ringing had restarted.

'Saving your wounded!'

'We have no *dee*-fence!' he screamed. 'We are nayk'd!'

'Nayk'd?'

What was he on about? It was beyond her. Except that she felt he grudgingly approved.

''Nayk'd!'

He said nothing more. Grabbing her arm, he rushed her forwards along the clinker beside the line. She saw what he intended. The train was beginning to move, not jerking this time but creeping forward with leviathan slowness as the locomotive's wheels raced on the snow-slippery rails and steam jetted upwards. He managed to grab hold of a handrail and haul Alice after him on to the crowded rear platform of the second carriage. For a moment she swung away from him, her feet finding no grip, and then the accelerating movement of the train drew her back towards him and, though hanging outwards at a slight angle, she managed to grab hold of part of the rear railing with her free hand and find somewhere for her feet.

The ground below her was moving, sleeper after sleeper, snow whirling up towards her as if coming through the wheels, and the flakes dashed at her with increasing strength just like a baby's soft hands beating happily, joyously, lovingly into a mother's face. Behind her she glimpsed men in greatcoats running beside the train. As it began to gather speed, she saw them cast aside their weapons and spring on to whatever purchase they could find on the sides or backs of the wagons.

What on earth had she done? She had done only what her conscience dictated. She had saved wounded men instead of horses. And she had done it spontaneously, by good luck, by mistake, by sheer effrontery. The thought made her shake. She started shaking so much she felt she might let go of the railing. Her teeth were chattering. But she was seized by an inner certainty she had done what she should have done and she would never have been able to forgive herself if she had not done what she did. She was sure of herself now, sure of her love, sure of her life, sure of being truly free. This spontaneous act was a defiant closure, a completeness that erased the past from her heart.

Naked!

Of course! That's what he was saying!

Then like a sunburst the sky behind them ignited. The black side of the adjacent wagon sprang sharply into view. Beyond it the huge, black, rectangular shapes of following wagons swayed in slow-motion silhouette. Everything was lit up whitely as in an over-exposed photograph. Even the black smoke pouring from the ammunition fire acquired a greyer tinge, lit as it was from below by the explosion of white light. A second later the dark returned, but through it came a torrent of exploding sound and a shudder of the air. In terror she heaved herself up farther on to the rear platform, yelling in such fright she knew she had never yelled like that before in her life.

12

Around her was the hot, sticky, smelly warmth of the carriage and a falsely bright light as if seen through tissue paper due to the sun shining horizontally in the window. She had been in a dream of riding in a different carriage through Central Park. Her father was taking off his hat to a woman riding by. Her mother was opposite her, her mouth fixed in a straight line, unsmiling. The sun had shone very brightly in her eyes.

'*Open your parasol, dear*,' her mother said. Her mother's round, kindly, lined face, with the shapely lips of the wide, mobile mouth and the extraordinarily beautiful clear brown eyes had looked down at her. They became brimful of tears. 'No, no, mother, please,' she had said. 'I am only twelve, but I know, you know, I really do know.' '*Open your parasol, dear*,' her mother had said.

It was none of her business. They had gone to Paris and then to London. Her mother had said it was better than New York. Her mother's eyes and voice had been the moving components of a dream that had run on and on, on and on until, with a pang of terror, she felt the motion had stopped.

It had stopped. She was awake and the train had stopped.

For several moments she tried to adjust her eyes to what she was seeing. People were pressed so tightly up against her on the wooden seat she felt she simply couldn't move. She saw people crammed on the luggage racks above her head and others lying in the central corridor. Frost on the carriage windows gave the bright round sun a furry, yellowish edge. It took her a while to remember exactly where she was and what had happened the previous night.

She was beside Leo. How she got to be beside him she could not remember except that now he was awake and her mother's dream face had melted into his and he was looking at her with features made as radiant by the sunlight as a newly painted icon. From his broad forehead beneath his fur hat to the curve of eyebrow and shining eyes and lips slowly parting in the midst of his new growth of dark beard he possessed the kind of mysteriously protective authority she had admired when she first saw him.

'Where are we?'

He replied in a whisper, indicating the need for quietness.

'North of Mukden.'

'Are we at a station?'

'No.'

'Where then?'

'I don't know. We've been stopped about ten minutes.'

'Maybe it needs more water.'

'Maybe.'

It was trivially comforting to prattle on about such matters rather than ask about his injury, the pain of which did not seem to show in his face. In any case, the colour had returned to it overnight and she felt reassured.

A certain amount of soft whispering talk had begun elsewhere. Holes were rubbed in the frosty glass to see out, but no voice came from anywhere in the carriage announcing what might be seen and the uncertainty surrounding the reasons for the standstill left Alice equally wondering how she had come to be beside Leo, still consumed as she was by the reality of her dream. He dispersed it by saying quite loudly:

'You are angel of mercy.'

'Me?'

'You remember what you did?'

'I said the wounded should come first.'

'Kozlov, Nikki Kozlov, our leader at present – all our destinies are in his hands – he said "Miss May, you are ang-*el* of mercy!" He said you were right. Apart from some orderlies, the nursing staff had left earlier, you see. It is what he called you – "ang-*el* of mercy".'

The woman opposite leaned forward and, to Alice's astonishment, kissed the back of her fur-gloved hand, made the sign of the cross and smiled broadly.

'*Blago-de-tel-nitsa.*'

The whispered word acknowledged an almost religious gratitude. It pleased her to be called a benefactress and yet she was puzzled by the show of affection. Both feelings were no doubt visible in her face as she turned and saw the admiring ovals of Leo's blue-emerald eyes, a shade darker than she remembered them, looking at her with such a calm, unblinking perusal.

'Why did she say that?'

'You really do not remember?'

'I was very indignant, I know that. I was angry that the wounded were being left behind.'

He responded in a pleasantly ironic tone. 'You are our heroine. It is very suitable, yes, very suitable. In our present uncertain times.' A mannered wistfulness almost expunged the irony and yet, accompanied by a sad smile, left no doubt about his sincere gratitude and respect. 'You see, our Nikki Kozlov had orders. He must embark cavalry horses to protect – what is it? I forget – oh, yes, *rearguard*. Our *rearguard* is now not protected. You have upset plans - very good plans - of Russian High Command. But then Japanese have also upset very good plans.' His whispering assumed a mock gravity. 'Perhaps what you did will be successful. It can mean winning war for us, you know. Our generals cannot and perhaps you can.'

Busy whisperings had arisen throughout the carriage. The woman opposite was busily whispering to her companion and a young mother with a baby to her breast was cooing in the compartment's far corner. For several instants Alice smiled to herself at the irony of Leo's words. She then thought quite domestically and practically about the need for breakfast. Until she distinctly heard gunfire. It was very close.

Everyone stiffened. The baby, withdrawn from the nipple, began to cry. The mother quickly drew the baby back to her but her own shock had stopped the flow of milk and the baby was crying again very shortly. Two small children beside her started whimpering.

A torrent of bullets suddenly swept along the far side of the train, thudding into woodwork and smashing windows.

Panic was unstoppable. There was a burst of shrieking women's voices and children's cries. Before Alice could even get to her feet she saw people already dashing from the train. Doors had been pulled open on their side and people were scrambling out as best they could. With his right hand Leo managed to get their door open quick enough to allow the two small children to be handed out, before a further burst of machine-gun fire sent a hail of bullets along the far side of the train.

This time the mother with the baby was hit. She had stood up, her mouth wide open, her arms fixed in a cradling gesture in front of her, but to Alice's horror the baby fell out of the arms in a gradual tumble of tight swaddling and came to rest beside one of the previously whispering women, its pale face with wide-open mouth and eyes staring upwards in perplexity and astonishment for one silent instant. Then all the tiny features puckered themselves up into a gathering misery of recrimination. The mother collapsed back on to the wooden seat and blood flowed out of her mouth. Leo rushed to her but she was dead.

'Down! Down!'

The cry was hardly necessary. Another burst of gunfire sent more bullets thudding into the side of the train, smashing doors and windows, and brought a shower of glass down on Alice's head as she crouched in a foetal position under the wooden seat. She was simply shaking with such fear she could scarcely catch her breath. The baby, now above her, broke out crying again. The two women who had been whispering scrambled on all fours in a fast scuttling motion along the central corridor, paying no attention to the cries for help from farther down the carriage.

Alice did the first thing that occurred to her. She stretched up and snatched off the seat the bundle of swaddling that was the baby. Her terrified shaking somehow had a calming effect on the little thing. She saw Leo's face peer round at her and read in it all she wanted to know. She had to force herself to get out of the death trap of the train. Clutching the baby to her with one hand, she crawled as quickly as she could into the central corridor, blocked, as she saw, by a bulky fur-clad male body that turned out to be an officer's over which she scrambled in a panic-driven frenzy and then climbed to her feet and ran out on to the rear platform.

The sun was blinding. Equally sunlit, but strangely crouched and sprawled about, were dozens of people using the embankment as cover. Someone signalled to her to come down. She rushed down the steps from the rear platform and threw herself literally into the arms of a woman lying there quivering and crossing herself. The baby tumbled into these arms and seemed to lodge there.

Leo was still on the train, she felt sure, yet her own panic made her totally will-less for a moment. All she could do was crouch and shake and keep her eyes tight shut. She dared not even look at the people round her. Heroine, indeed! she thought.

No one moved. Two sharp explosions shattered the quiet of the morning. They were followed by two or three more. She opened her eyes and saw people exchanging glances. Should they run? The open, snow-dusted emptiness of the land extending away from them to the east, with nothing to be seen in the sunlight except telegraph poles marching starkly north and south into invisibility, offered less hope of safety than the embankment. Some people had tried to take cover there, but the outline of their shapes was obvious.

'*Grana-a-ty*!'

The word was pronounced with a crunching of saliva by someone close by. Grenades! Grenades had been thrown!

Everyone waited. No one spoke. There was an intense quietness as if they were all hiding in a room ready to surprise someone. Only the locomotive regularly emitted steam like a large animal breathing. Then came one or two shouts. Some bolder spirits raised their heads high enough to peer above the rails and see what was happening. Apparently the machine-gun had been captured.

Crouched down but running, the skirt of his long coat touching the ground, came Nikki Kozlov, gesturing for everyone to keep their heads down. Several other men followed him, two of them carrying the captured weapon and another a long ammunition belt looped over his shoulder. Among this group of running, crouching men Alice saw Oliver. He was dressed now in an officer's fur hat too large for him so that it came down almost to his eyes and, tied to his head by a scarf, gave him the comic appearance of an extremely elderly woman with a young boy's face. She called out to him and he came breathlessly up to her.

'Were they grenades? Who threw them?' she asked.

He looked at her with such a concerned, unusual gaze she thought he had not recognised her. He reached out one hand – he was wearing a mitten – and touched the bandage across her forehead with the tip of his right index finger in a gingery, tentative movement, showing her the blood on it when he drew back. She recoiled at the sight and at once felt the bandage herself. She had started bleeding again.

Still Oliver did not speak. He looked closely up into her face, blinking his eyes, and extracted from his pocket, as if it were a toy or a recent purchase in which he thought she might be interested, a pomegranate-shaped metal object and showed her with a movement of his mouth and bared teeth how he could pull out the pin. The sight of it in his hands made her freeze with fear. It was only the baby crying momentarily in the arms of the woman beside her, who was rocking it backwards and forwards, that released her from a sinister, paralysing sense of Oliver's strangeness. He had changed into a creature of the war, she thought, and lost his former attractive, unpretentious boyishness.

'Oliver dear, you know what that is, you...'

Very haughtily, reminding her of Elizabeth, he smiled and then nodded brusquely. He put the object back in his pocket.

'I threw one.'

'You did?'

'Yes'

They were whispering. People round them were stirring out of their panic and beginning to talk to each other.

'Nikki showed me what to do. We r-ran there...' He spoke briefly of having thrown a grenade at the Japanese machine-gun hidden in a building near the track. There was no boasting in what he said.

She could not rebuke him as she had done in his little attic room. Reaching out her arms impulsively, she held him so close it felt as if she wanted to squash him. She was astonished a little at her own strength. The recognition that he was now the only real connection she still had with her London past, the embodiment of her earlier, custodial life as the guardian of their long journey to China made her hug him all the more intensely.

'Dear Oliver, I wish I'd known you longer.'

Now why did she say that? She astonished herself by saying it, yet it was exactly what she meant. She had never known him sufficiently well. Holding him, she could sense the springy musculature, the physical latency of the man within him. He astonished her in his turn by saying:

'I want you to have something.'

'What?'

'This.'

He fished out of his pocket the intently marching lead soldier she had seen on his washstand.

'But I can't! What would I do with one of your soldiers?'

'He was my king. At home when I had all my soldiers. Please, Alice, have it. I'm a real soldier now, I don't need toys.'

He pressed it into her gloved hand and folded her fingers round it.

'Oh, my dear, no, no, no…'

He muttered something about Arina at that point, but Nikki Kozlov came running back and Oliver gently withdrew himself from her. He looked straight into her face, smiled at her and kissed her. The sweetness of the kiss evoked in a rush all the protectiveness and tenderness she had felt for him and for Elizabeth. They had shared so much, she thought. Yet she had never been close to him. As she had said, she wished she had known him longer and now all she had as a reminder was the toy soldier pressed into her hand as a keepsake.

Suddenly there was a general commotion all round her as people were ordered back on the train. From the rapid chatter of neighbours she gathered that no one had expected the Japanese to have penetrated as far north as this and it was therefore essential to join up with the columns of Russian troops retreating towards Harbin. That was the official version, as it were. More effective was the panic version which simply dictated that they should get away from the ambush site as soon as possible.

To Alice's relief she saw Leo re-appear on the rear platform of their carriage the instant the train started to move, helping people to scramble aboard with his uninjured right hand. The children of the dead mother were comforted by some of the women but everyone was ordered to lie down and share the floor space with the dead and injured, among the shattered woodwork and the glass shards. A general state of shock affected them all. An irrepressible, hysterical wailing came intermittently from one of the compartments. To Alice the sound exactly matched her own shiverings and sudden bouts of violently chattering teeth.

Inch by inch the train crept forward. No one knew at first why it was going at such a snail's pace. Then the grapevine of whispers brought news that the line ahead was being kept under continual scrutiny for any signs of activity by Japanese sappers. This was what had caused the first stoppage.

In such a landscape the train was an obvious target. Alice could see how the nearly horizontal sun made the shadows of the rolling stock and wheels elongate across the frozen millet fields like bars of shadow running across crumpled sheets. As a target, it had at all costs to keep on the move, just as its occupants had to cling to the hope that the Japanese machine-gun was no more than a fluke. A reconnaissance detachment, so Leo suggested as he and Alice crouched in the carriage doorway.

'God help us, let us hope it is not Japanese army. What could we do if one whole army was here?'

They kept their eyes skinned for any sign of human movement in the flat, snow-flecked countryside. Unspoken though it was, the knowledge that they were travelling in what amounted to a slow cortege of wheeled coffins was the worst fear. Unceremoniously, efficiently and quickly, the dead, including the baby's mother, were collected up and moved to a single compartment set aside for them. Alice helped with this until she felt so exhausted she had to rest.

There was still an urgent need to look after the recently injured and the wounded in the wagons at the back. Neither she nor Leo could trust themselves to use the footplates and handholds on the sides of the wagons, so they joined the end wagon by stepping down and letting the slow moving train pass along the track. The strafing had caused less damage here. A young officer sitting astride a wagon buffer helped her and Leo up. He had binoculars and was surveying the countryside to the west as, minute by minute, more features became visible and the likelihood of further attack more obvious.

What could they do? It was Nikki Kozlov talking as he stood by one of the ramps in the end wagon half lowered to let in daylight. Anxious and pale, with fine lines of tiredness tautening the skin round his still ultra-bright eyes, he spoke his thoughts aloud. They could not leave the train now. So long as the line was clear, they should keep moving. But the smoke would be visible for miles. Should they leave the wounded in the wagons? It was a civilian train, after all. They could not protect themselves. Seeing Alice, he broke into English.

'Miss May, we are nayk'd! No hors-*es*! What do we do? We are nayk'd!'

Naked!

She could not help smiling. The last thing, of course, anyone would want to be in the ice cold of this Manchurian plain was naked. Conceivably, had they been able to deploy cavalry at this stage of their journey, they might have been able to reconnoitre beyond the immediate environs of the track. That was obvious. It would have been a dubious form of protection, however, if there really were a Japanese army out there.

He was too carried away to notice her smile. He engaged in a little tirade against the way in which the best advice of those with experience and knowledge had been ignored by the High Command. Now it was the duty of those charged with the task of saving the honour of the Great Russian people to show greater vigilance than ever.

His words should have struck echoes of accord in every heart. That they didn't was not his fault. He knew as well as anyone that it cheered people to hear criticism of the Russian generals who had served them so badly throughout the Manchurian campaign. As for the honour of the Great Russian people and the call to vigilance, it seemed to have less appeal. Alice saw the men deliberately turn their heads. Some spat, others morosely smoked. The rhetoric simply made Leo chortle.

Whether or not Oliver understood it, she was not sure. He stood there proudly beside Nikki looking, despite his bedraggled appearance and outsize hat, a splendidly upright and alert lieutenant. The train, though, was defenceless, there was no denying it. The captured machine-gun had been set up on the rear platform of the second carriage. Otherwise few of the troops apart from the officers seemed to be carrying weapons. Oliver himself may have kept his grenade, but his main concern was Arina.

What he had tried to tell Alice was that she was ill with the same fever that had struck down Leo. He took her to see the girl. Shivering, she crouched among straw, her eyes glittering and her face now transformed into a peeky replica of its former rosy freshness. Takeo-san had insisted on looking after her. She gave Alice a faint smile of recognition and then leaned back with her eyes closed and let the train rock her gently to and fro, Oliver beside her.

Takeo-san's loyalty to the Russian nurse as to other wounded was never questioned. It was assumed he was one of the Chinese orderlies from the Mission who had elected to stay with the Russians during the retreat. Other medical orderlies tried to help as best they could, but self-help and vodka had become the only effective cures. Cold though the wagons were, there was a preference for travelling with the ramps partly open or lashed to the outside of the wagons so long as the sun shone and the vodka was passed round. By slow degrees the train gathered speed.

It went from a walking pace to the equivalent of a jogging run and then a canter. Rocked to and fro, most wounded huddled together for warmth, glad of the faint heat of the sun on their faces and the sense that each click of the wheels on the rails or telegraph post going by meant a further short stage in the retreat from war. Alice stepped among them, able to do no more than offer sympathy, but the way they reached up to her, kissed her hands, even the skirt of her coat, alarmed her a little by its very demonstrativeness. When they begged her to stay with them in the end wagon, she and Leo found places leaning on one of the half open ramps facing the sun.

Where are we going? It was not a question she had bothered to ask aloud. Now Leo, his right arm round her again, read her thoughts. He spoke into a flow of cool air.

'We will start again. You and I.'

'Where?'

'Where I can be free.' What did he mean? He meant he had to go to Moscow first. 'My mother is very ill. I heard about it three days ago.'

She nodded, her eyes momentarily blinded by the sunlight.

'I must go to her as soon as I can.'

'Yes, I understand.'

'I must arrange these things. Afterwards where? You and I, where do we go? Do we go to New York?'

'New York,' she said dreamily. 'Home.'

In the rattle of the train, with the Manchurian sun in her face, she spoke as if a magic carpet would waft them there. New York at such a moment seemed the airiest of castles on the farthest of horizons. It was as if the vagueness of her dream had once more enveloped her.

'You know what will happen...' She was talking to herself, her thoughts turning once again to her mother and the reasons for leaving New York, how there had been so many governesses, so many teachers, and finally such a lot to do when her mother was ill in the London house, now apparently sold, so her father said in his letter. 'I will be going home to my father. I will say to him: Here is my husband, the famous, courageous and very talented Russian surgeon, Dr Leo Nikitin. A New York hospital will be bound to want to employ him. And my father will say: 'Welcome to our family, Dr Leo! If my daughter has chosen you as her husband, I am sure she has made the right choice. New York. We go home.'

He picked up on her meaning, smiling into her face.

'So, my dear, do we say *we* now? All our lives do we say *we*?'

The train wheels gave a jump. Alice saw the black smoke form a line of small, diminishing puffs against a pale-blue sky, glassy now and cloudless after the recent storms. The feeling returned strongly that so long as they were moving they would be safe. More strongly still she felt the assurance arising from his questions. She thought of them as expressing in their simplicity the same crystal brilliance of the sky, touched by nothing except the fingerprints of black smoke. The fingerprints vanished away one by one and left only the clean surface of the sky as immaculate as freshly washed glass,

'Yes,' she said. 'It will be we, Dr and Mrs Nikitin....'

His shoulders shook slightly with silent laughter.

*

This time she felt the impact on her eardrums. The explosion was shattering. Before she was properly awake she was already on her feet and the earth beside the track was coming up at her as she sprang from the wagon. All she could be certain about was that Leo was there as well. Side by side they scrambled down the shallow embankment and jumped a ditch and went some way up the stony, rutted expanse of a millet field and fell flat on their faces as two more explosions burst round them, filling the air with fountains of earth that showered down stones and ice-hard fragments of soil. They struck her head and back in sharp fistfuls as if she were being deliberately attacked and she felt resentful. She found herself spitting out bits of earth and at the same time shivering and whimpering and yet still unsure whether she were awake or not.

They were on higher ground. The landscape was no longer flat. Behind and in front of them was an upland rising towards the foothills of what appeared to be distant mountains. They could see the train was in a kind of shallow valley. Dozens of people had fled from it after the first explosion. They were lying now or crouching in its vicinity. Clearly visible were the outlines of the rolling stock, some windows lowered in the front carriages, some broken and some of the wagons with ramp doors open so that the land on the far side gleamed palely through the rectangular holes. To all intents and purposes the train suddenly appeared uninhabited. No sentries or lookouts could be seen and the only movement was the smoke rising steadily from the locomotive stack.

It was then Alice caught sight of men moving on the other side of the valley. She could not judge how far away they were but they could clearly be seen as soldiers advancing with fixed bayonets, the steel sparkling in the sunlight. They were coming down the shallow, undulant slope in fits and starts, not in steady lines, so that they would disappear at intervals, only to reappear again where the folds of the land offered no concealment. They seemed to know that the train was at their mercy.

The anonymity of these figures, their presence not as a visible, human enemy but as something impersonal like encroaching water, struck Alice forcibly. They were an advancing army, although not sufficiently identifiable to seem really hostile. The shelling or mortaring had now stopped and a silence filled with nothing except a busy, rather excited birdsong replaced it. Again

Alice could not be sure whether this was really some form of birdsong or a singing in her ears from the explosions.

She felt exposed, '*nayk'd,*' she told herself, out in this area of stony upland. There was no cover, nowhere at all to hide. She found the situation too terrible to contemplate and so lay there and shivered with her eyes closed. The Japanese *were* there. All the hopes of the machine-gunner being a fluke were nonsense. They were cut off and it was only a matter of time before they were captured. Or killed. It reminded her of what she had only known at second hand, the fact that this war between Russians and Japanese had been fought at an unprecedented level of savagery. It was a fact she wanted to close her eyes against, to shut out, as she had shut other things from her life. So she shut her eyes and shut out New York and her father and the future and listened and waited.

Suddenly Leo gave her a nudge. She opened her eyes. He was drawing her attention to something while simultaneously trying not to move. She followed his gaze as best she could. A figure had become visible in silhouette on the rear platform of the second carriage. It was where the captured machine-gun had been positioned. They watched as the figure crouched over the weapon and aimed it towards the approaching Japanese.

A burst of fire quickly ensued. Spent cartridge cases flew up in a little arc. Perhaps a score or so of rounds were discharged, followed by silence. Alice expected the figure to take cover. Or perhaps whoever it was did not realize how conspicuous he was. But there was no further movement from the figure and no further firing. For a fleeting second or so the incident seemed to be over. The busily singing birds had fallen quiet once again, as if listening like the rest of them for the next noise to shatter the morning. Instead, a little to her surprise, Alice distinctly saw a flash from the far land opposite. Then came the sharp crack of a rifle shot, followed by another, and as if in slow motion the figure by the machine-gun seemed to pirouette on the narrow area of the rear platform, one arm flung upwards and outwards, and, lifted slightly in the air, spinning, the figure fell. It was then Alice saw the strange headgear tied with a scarf fall away and knew who it was.

She was up on her feet and running at once. The slope of the stony field seemed to give her a fleetness that lifted her up and made the sensation of running almost unconscious. All she noticed was one small crater left by one of the explosions and dodged round it. People crouching or lying closer to the train called to her to get down, but she ran straight towards where the body was and as she came close and fell on her knees beside it she knew she had not been wrong. It was Oliver's body.

The outsize officer's fur hat had been shaken away and he was lying there with his tawny blond hair drawn back and his young face staring up. The bullets had apparently struck him in the heart so that, though his shirt beneath the greatcoat was red with blood, his features, with his mouth a little open and his eyes looking up brightly, were immaculate and unspoiled and left her sure for an instant he was alive. She put both hands down to touch either side of his face as if she were going to wake him. The blood did not spurt, it oozed. She held her hands to his cheeks in a gesture of affection, shaking her head to and fro in reproach. You should not have done that, Oliver dear, she thought. It was *so* silly of you. Knowing enough to realize there was nothing to revive, she withdrew her hands. In any case, *this* was not the Oliver she had hugged so recently. *This* was someone much younger, a boy she should have protected, a child she had promised to look after.

The realization caused a sharp physical pain like a knife thrust. It was a paralysing pain, taking away her breath and freezing her will. Though she knew Leo had joined her and had leaned over and closed Oliver's eyes, she had no ears for his words and scarcely seemed to notice his efforts to lift her to her feet. Nor did she realize he was trying to draw her away not just from Oliver, but also from the Japanese troops who had already appeared on the far side of the track and were approaching the train. So when she stood up suddenly, almost pushing Leo to one side, she was confronted by lines of bayonets only a few feet away. The sight was meaningless to her. She was moved by the continuing pain in another direction, down the line of black wagons with their pitched roofs, past the open doors, stumbling over the stones among the sleepers. Leo followed after her and helped her, continually asking her why, why, why was she doing what she was doing, and she paid no attention to him. Then she asked to be helped to mount the end wagon.

Arina was still crouching there in the corner where she had been. Alice knelt beside her and took her hand. The girl tried to raise her head but Alice made her lie back. It had already dawned on her, she thought.

13

There came a loud banging on the side of the wagon. Rifle butts were being used to attract attention. Alice looked out and saw soldiers waving angrily, signalling for the occupants to come down. At the same time she knew the floor space of the wagon contained at least a dozen wounded men who would certainly not be able to alight of their own accord and among them, she suspected, were some who were already dead. Leo was standing on the track verge when she looked out. He glanced up at her and held up his arms in an offer to help her down. At that instant she caught sight of Takeo-san who had shed his parka and was dressed in his white medical coat. The men in the wagon were beseeching her to help them.

'Takeo-san!' she called out. 'Takeo-san!'

He looked up at her. She knew he had to make a difficult choice since it was his chance to return to his own people.

'Tell them!' she shouted. 'Tell them it is a train full of wounded men! Tell them we are only civilians! Tell them to let us go!'

There was a rustling of straw among the wounded behind her but no one spoke. Few if any of them understood her words and she was uncertain why she was being so bold.

'Tell them!'

Rifle butts were still being hammered against the wooden sides of the wagons to the accompaniment of incomprehensible, guttural commands from a Japanese officer.

'Tell them!'

She thought it was futile. Her voice could scarcely make itself heard above the other noises and she was finding it so painful to yell she felt limp from the effort. She sank to her knees in the doorway of the wagon.

Then came Takeo-san's voice. Whatever he said, it had a quite sudden effect. The Japanese officer marched towards him, giving every impression of being about to strike him, and then he stopped in his tracks, drew himself upright and gave a smart bow. Takeo spoke thinly but slowly and commandingly. The officer bowed again and then stepped back smartly and saluted.

The banging of the rifle butts stopped. Instead Alice was faced by a couple of Japanese soldiers who clambered agilely into the wagon and began a minute inspection of the wounded men. They stepped carefully among them, poking with their bayonets at the few pieces of baggage, lifting blankets, gingerly sniffing vodka bottles or flasks if they found them. To Alice and Arina they were courteous, but they still insisted on patting their clothing meticulously for concealed weapons. Only one revolver was discovered among the wounded and it was flung out on to the earth beside the track.

Hardly much more was found in other wagons. The captured machine-gun was quickly taken away. Nikki Kozlov and a dozen or so other Russian officers and sentries were lined up and stripped of their arms in full view of everyone on the train. The sight provoked some remarks among men peering out of the doorway. They were bound to be shot, one voice pronounced sombrely. Leo had scrambled aboard when he had the chance once the Japanese left the wagon and signed for the man to stop. It was obvious to everyone now that the

Chinese Eastern Railway was no longer in Russian hands, retreat northwards was unlikely and they were in danger of being ordered back to Mukden.

As Alice watched, there came the noise of horses' hooves and a couple of armed men rode up, bringing their charges to a straight-legged halt right in front of the Japanese officer and the line of disconsolate Russians. Bows, salutes, staccato commands and further exchanges marked their arrival, with one of the riders springing to the ground and, bowing, passing across what appeared to be a despatch.

Self-importantly, evidently prolonging the protocol to which he was entitled, the officer took his time in ordering a subordinate to hold out the document for him to read. He placed pince-nez on his nose. Several seconds of relative quiet ensued while he read. Then he abruptly straightened his back. An instant later he began waving frantically.

In an astonishing reversal, the whole train, it now seemed, had assumed a role of little more importance than an annoying traffic problem. It had to be got out of the way as soon as possible. The officer signalled for the locomotive crew to return and everyone else to board it. Scarcely believing their good fortune, Nikki Kozlov and his group raced for the front carriages and in seconds were clambering aboard the end platforms.

With a jerk and a racing of the locomotive's wheels the train moved forward. Panic clearly governed the crew's actions. For a moment of breath-holding torment it seemed the locomotive would stall, but steam rose upwards in a great jet and buffers clanged one against another as the rolling stock was shunted together by the jerky start and men swayed dangerously in the doorways. Leo, his left arm firmly jammed through one of the boltholes for the ramps, leaned down and with his free hand seized the hand of the running Takeo-san and swept him up into the wagon despite a last-minute attempt by one of the Japanese soldiers to detain him. Gasping and grinning, with a kind of totter, he staggered into the interior of the wagon and came to a halt almost face to face with Alice. She held out her arms to him, kneeling as she was, and said:

'Bushi! Bushi!'

The metallic drumming of the wheels quickly accelerated from a slow, funereal beat into the beginnings of a tattoo. She leaned in the doorway, still kneeling, and there, beside the track, as the train described a slow, curving arc, she saw Oliver's body. The pale white face and fair hair emitted a kind of glimmer against the brown earth. Silently tears streamed down her cheeks and into her open mouth.

She had not looked after him.

She inhaled a long, shuddering, tearful breath. Oh, Ollie dear, how silly! She found the silk handkerchief, her 'Alice' handkerchief with the 'A' embroidered in one corner. It was spotted with drops of her blood, now gone rust-red and stiff. Slowly she wiped her eyes.

In the far distance, just where Oliver's body was still lying, she saw the Japanese beginning to lay charges to the rails. Theirs was the last train, just as he had said.

*

She lay beside Arina in the straw and held her hand. That was enough comfort for her. She scarcely knew the girl, but she sensed intuitively that there had been more than a simple tenderness between her and Oliver. Men did not really know how to give comfort at a time like this. Men simply did not have the delicacy. She and the girl were joined now in a common bereavement and could be soft and delicate in their grief. The world of men, of the train's rocking, swaying motion and the groans of some of the wounded, the babblings of one delirious man, the smell of *mahorka*, the cranking clatter of some brake lever striking on a ratchet, the chill breezes blown in through the open doorways but preferable to the stench if the ramps were raised – this world of men had to be fended off and softened and made sweet, and the only way Alice thought of doing this was by lying beside the girl and holding her hand and letting the pain of her grief run its course through her as the noise of the train and its motion seemed unending.

She must have slept. She did not know how long. A cradling sensation induced by the lullaby of the beating wheels left her floating. She was able to look down and watch someone, a woman like her, lying on a beach as a tide withdrew, watching the smallest wavelets vanish into sand, feeling pangs of hunger as normality returned and surprising herself by a certainty that her memory of Mukden, the American Mission and all the people she had known displaced the need for grief. It would be replaced, she told herself. It was a certainty reinforced by a new spirit in what she saw round her, mostly by an awareness of Leo's closeness. His strength and warmth beside her softened the jolts from the wagon.

Men had gathered in the open doorways again. They were exchanging shouts with others outside. Two or three were lying supine, their faces covered with blankets. She knew they were the dead. It was strange now how she took it for granted. Never before in her life had she felt how right it was that the dead should be there among the living. But now the train was not a hearse, it began to seem an ark of salvation in which most of the wounded were either leaning on one elbow or sitting upright or managing to stand. Even Arina had managed to draw herself up into a sitting position with her back propped against the side of the wagon.

'We've caught up,' Leo said. He spoke in Russian in a husky, tired whisper. 'They're ours out there. We've lost the war, of course. Russia, the colonial power, is no more. And perhaps there'll be no more Tsar.'

What *was* he talking about? *Bolshe ne budet...* He was a great talker, she knew that, and when he went on to talk about war as the slowest time of all and peace as always travelling much faster she recognised he was obviously still feverish. The softness of his voice speaking in her ear as the men went on exchanging shouts with other men beside the track brought her a reassuring sense that life would continue and perhaps, as he said, grow faster and faster through their loving contentment. He was looking at her. Moment by moment bolts of light through the open doorways lit up his eyes. She leaned towards him and kissed him on his bearded cheek.

'I know you loved that poor Oliver,' he said softly in Russian. 'I can mourn him, of course. He wanted to be a hero, but then every man alive, if he is honest, wishes to be a hero. I wanted it, too. But, yes, he made an attempt. Our writer Maxim Gorky celebrated "the madness of the brave" as "living wisdom" and that is how we should remember him. There is another wisdom, though. The men know it and I know it. I know I must be loyal to my friends, and Takeo-san is one of them. He has saved us. He and I, we go together.'

'I know, I know...'

'So where I go, he must go. That is our "living wisdom." But the men, they respect your "madness of the brave." Have you heard what they're saying?'

'No.'

'Then don't be surprised.'

The train, she realized, had been passing other wagons and carriages on an adjoining track and was drawing to a halt. Although she had heard Harbin mentioned in the conversation round her, she was uncertain whether they had reached it. Leo's question seemed too obvious to require an answer and yet it astonished her to find him already on his feet and lifting her up towards him.

'They are saying you, you alone, have won the war for them. You,' he announced, 'are a woman who won a war, you, the *Amerikanka,* you have saved them, that's what they're saying. It is true, you know.'

'Oh, no.' She shook her head.

'Yes. Listen.'

All she could hear was an incoherent roar of voices. Shouts broke out in muddled, disturbed choruses amongst the men in the wagon and were repeated outside by other voices. When she found herself drawn forward into the open doorway the noise of yells and whoops coming from scores of mouths outside made her think of a bubbling cauldron of voices floating on the surface of a mass of raised faces. They were raised unexpectedly and a little frighteningly towards her.

Once in the doorway she seemed to become the focus of their attention and she began to discern the sound of her own name.

'All I did was...' She turned to Leo in alarm.

'You saved them,' she heard him whisper close to her ear. 'They want to thank you. Don't be modest!'

With a long-drawn, nearly pleading summons, her name was being called by men below her on a station platform, by men pressing up against the train as it drew to a halt, by others in adjacent wagons. Quickly the sound beat in chorusing waves against her.

'*Al-y-y-ysa*! *Al-y-y-ysa*! *Al-y-y-ysa*!'

She could not help herself. She smiled. The calls grew more frenzied. They merged into another sound:

'*Ly-y-y-samerika-a-a-nka*! *Ly-y-y-samerik-a-anka*!'

She was lifted up on to someone's shoulder and carried off the wagon. Try as she might to stay with Leo, they would not let her. She had become some sort of prize for men released from the discipline of war, no longer *her* wounded, as she thought of them, no longer *her* wounded who remained largely on the train, but men now whistling and clapping their hands above their heads and cheering and continually shouting. There was such a crowd of them she found each raised, bearded face, each fur hat or forage cap shaken towards her, each pair of smiling, glowing eyes a blur, but a sparkling blur, like the sharp little explosive blurs of light that sunlight makes on ice.

And that is exactly what they were. Because her eyes had filled with tears and she could see nothing clearly. They were all tear-blurred, these men. It was a world fill of such tearful blurs. And buffeted, shaken, she was carried slowly on strong shoulders past her wagon to the next and at each open doorway there were bandaged, blood-stained, pale-faced blurs of men waving and calling to her:

'*Al-y-y-ysa*! *Amerik-a-a-anka*! *Al-y-y-ysa*! *Amerik-a-a-nka*!'

She waved back. She knew her cheeks were glistening wet. Her bandage had loosened and she tried to fix it while still waving. Still the strange cries resounded. Hands reached up to her.

Why me? she kept on wondering. What have I done? Don't be modest! she kept on hearing Leo whisper in her ear. So perhaps she had done something after all. She, an American girl, only a couple of generations away from slavery, who had landed up in the middle of a war more or less by accident, had found herself able to help by nursing and being friendly. She had done more or less what she'd been told to do and maybe love had helped, but – no, sir! - she was no Joan of Arc. Perhaps by just being who she was she had changed the course of things a little. She had insisted on wounded, not horses. She had made Takeo-san speak out on their behalf. Maybe it was because of being Alice May, that's all. Nothing else.

There she was, floating. Buoyant cries of her name rose to her like bouquets. The love around her matched all the love with which her heart was bursting. She was lifted up and floating on the bubbles of their cries. Every cry of '*Al-y-y-ysa*!' lifted her up higher and brought more tears of love to her eyes and blurred the men's faces for her and rang with relief and gratitude at having been saved from war.

At each cry of her name she waved the blood-stained handkerchief and let the tears pour from her eyes and could not help herself, suddenly aware of new life within her, the first urgent sense of pregnancy and motherhood, smiling back and repeating to herself in her heart, if not out loud, 'I love you! I love you!' as if each heartbeat, each indrawn breath, formed the words that were never likely to be heard in all the shouts and cries rising to her in huge waves of sound:

'*Al-y-y-sa*! *Amerika-a-anka*! *Urra*! *Urra*! *Aly-y-y-sa-a-a*! *Amerika-a-anka*! *Urra-a-a*! *Urra-a-a*!'

And so she was carried along shoulder-high from wagon to wagon.

Made in the USA
Monee, IL
28 April 2026